Published by
Nicky Charles and Jan Gordon

In the Cards
Copyright © 2018, 2015 by Nicky Charles and Jan Gordon
Ingram Paperback Edition

Canadian grammar was used in this book, hence you might notice some punctuation and spelling variations.

This book contains mature content and is intended for mature readers.

This book is a work of fiction and any resemblance to persons, living or dead, or places, events or locales is purely coincidental. The characters are productions of the authors' imagination and used fictitiously.

Edited by Jan Gordon and Nicky Charles
Line edits by Moody Edits

Cover by Patricia Schmitt (Pickyme)
Angel logo Copyright © Doron Goldstein, Designer

ISBN: 978-1-989058-22-0

IN THE CARDS

Nicky Charles
&
Jan Gordon

ACKNOWLEDGEMENTS

We'd like to thank our wonderful Beta readers:
Carmen, Kalia, Shirley, Tonya, Judy, Janet, Norma and Amy.
Your input was invaluable!

Also a huge 'thank you' goes to Janet.
Without her video talents we would be totally lost!

This book is dedicated to

QUENTIN

As the only man on our Street Team we value your input immensely. Your artistic talents also help us run Nicky's Facebook page smoothly. Thank you.

- Nicky & Jan

In the Cards

Prologue

Alex stifled a yawn as he opened his locker and hung his coat on a hook inside. White crystals glistened on the surface of the material before slowly disappearing as the warmth of the room dissolved them into droplets of water. It was snowing outside, the air crispy cool. Not enough though to dispel the tiredness that wrapped itself around him. He'd spent a restless night, unable to sleep; a situation that plagued him all too often of late. There was nothing particular on his mind, no worries keeping him awake. Even the upcoming meeting with his supervisor wasn't a real concern. True, he and Michael were often at odds but it wasn't something that had ever bothered him before. It was just…

He searched his mind for a cause then gave a mental shrug. A phase of random sleeplessness. Everyone had them.

The gleam of his halo sitting on the shelf caught his eye. It shimmered, the light emitting from it illuminated the small space making the angelic robes hanging on the hook below seem impossibly white. He hesitated over donning the headgear and mentally reviewed his recent actions. Basic routine, some paperwork, a few Earthly interventions. Nope, no rule transgressions…or at least none of any significance; there'd be no need to smooth the waters by appearing in formal gear. Michael's summons probably wasn't to ream him out over a minor folly. Most likely he was going to be given a new assignment.

Michael's communiqués were almost always cryptic. Some said it was his style but Alex suspected it was a management technique. The other man liked to keep his underlings guessing and on their toes. As for himself, Alex had been a guardian angel long enough that not much fazed him anymore. Whatever Michael had to say to him, it wouldn't be anything new.

Leaving his halo and the accompanying robes where they were, Alex closed the door and punched his timecard. Another workday had begun.

Some guardian angels, or GAs as they called themselves for the sake of brevity, lived full-time in Heaven and merely had to roll out of bed to be at work. He, however, preferred to maintain an apartment in the human realm. There was a bit of a commute but it kept him anchored. The experience of living as a regular man, albeit with the extra convenience of supernatural powers, helped him in his assignments. Humans were more complicated than some of his coworkers believed. Emotional, prone to impulsive actions, limited in life-span; theirs wasn't an easy lot. He'd been thinking just that this morning when he'd left his building and promptly stepped in a puddle of slush, soaking his sock and probably ruining his leather shoe.

The summons to appear in Heaven had buoyed his soggy spirits, providing an opportunity to escape the chill of an early northern winter. He hated the cold: hunching against the bitter wind which could cut through the warmest clothing like a finely tempered sword. Just the thought of icy ears and frozen fingers and toes had him shivering. It was the only downside to living in the human dimension. Unfortunately, his current area of operations was North America and unless he could arrange a transfer to somewhere tropical or even to one of the southern American states, he was stuck with snow and ice for the next three months.

"'Morning, Alex."

The greeting drew him from his introspection and he nodded in reply to the casual acquaintance, then held the door open for another angel to pass through. She absent-mindedly smiled her thanks, before hurrying down the hall. A newbie late for a meeting if he was any judge. Most likely she was wishing she could use her wings to speed her progress but didn't want to draw attention to her tardiness. He smiled, vague memories of his own early days as a guardian angel coming to mind.

Learning the etiquette of a new job wasn't always easy and Heaven was no different than any other workplace. There were certain dos and don'ts. Everyone had the ability to walk through walls and transport themselves instantly from one place to another but, unless it was an emergency, the occupants were expected to move around like regular humans. Unnecessary displays of angelic abilities were frowned upon lest they lead to grandstanding.

Alex pushed the button to summon the elevator and entered when the doors slid open, grateful the endless flights of marble stairs had been replaced with more modern conveniences. Heaven's physical appearance had evolved over the centuries just as the human world had. Technology had replaced parchment and quills. Sleek glass and steel now stood where stone pillars had once dominated. Change was the only constant in the universe no matter where one went.

Exiting the elevator, Alex walked the halls to his destination, nodding to others he knew. Some had arms laden with files; others seemed preoccupied with weighty problems. Heaven was a busy place; drifting about on clouds seldom happened.

Eventually, he arrived in an anteroom and sat down to wait to be called into the presence of his immediate superior. Soft classical music played in the background; a few magazines were neatly stacked on a coffee table. He ignored them, instead wondering again if he was about to be given a new assignment. If so, he hoped there'd be a bit of a challenge to it. His cases had all been pretty calm lately. Perhaps that was contributing to his sleep difficulties; there was nothing like a good day's work to help usher in the presence of the proverbial sandman.

Not that he was complaining about getting an easy job now and then. Being a GA was hard work and there was always the potential for danger lurking. Humans were so unpredictable. There were even stories—unfounded rumours no doubt—of guardians who failed to return from assignments. Alex strongly suspected the tales were fostered to reinforce the importance of following the rules laid out in the guardian angel handbook.

The inner door finally opened and a GA exited Michael's office, her eyes fixed on a picture taped to the front of a folder.

"Morning, Eugenie. New assignment?" Alex stood, nodding towards the folder she was carrying.

The woman made an indistinct sound in reply, her brow furrowed.

Alex took a moment to watch the normally talkative woman leave before heeding the implicit summons of the open door. If Eugenie's assignment could render her almost silent, what might his next job be like? Whatever it was, he'd handle it. Being a guardian angel was his life and he'd pledged to do whatever an assignment required of him.

Michael silently observed the GA who had entered the room, using that scant time frame to compose himself. He'd just given out an extremely difficult assignment, the details heart-wrenching. While he presented a calm façade to his employees, he wasn't immune to the emotional toll of the job. It would never do for the GAs to know that, however.

He pushed Eugenie's case from his mind and focused on Alex. Alexander Flint was one of his best men. Devoted to his job, clever; a man who thought on his feet and could handle a curve ball when it came at him out of nowhere. Yes, Alex was reliable despite the maverick streak that reared its head at times.

"Michael."

"Alex." He acknowledged the greeting and gave a nod indicating the other man should take a seat. The GA complied and Michael eased back in his own chair, allowing himself a moment to appreciate how the soft leather conformed to his contours. One of the perks of the job, though it hardly compensated for the weight of responsibility he carried. Managing a squadron of guardian angels wasn't for the faint of heart. So much depended on matching the right human to the right angel. A mistake on his part could have consequences that would have a domino effect down through the centuries. Like a house of cards, one person's life supported all those around it. If removed too soon, without proper precautions, the whole thing could collapse. Yet, conversely, too many cards in one place could have the same result. A balancing act, that's what it was.

Yes, the proper angel for the job... He eyed Alex, noting the faint shadows under his eyes. "How are things on Earth, Alex?"

"Same old, same old." The comment was accompanied by a one-shouldered shrug. "The weather is crappy in the northern states, half the human population have head colds and those who don't are already complaining about the holiday season. Thanksgiving is just around the corner and then there are the Christmas preparations they have to do. Seems there's always something stressing them out."

"Wearying of your neighbours? Would you like to have a room up here? It can be arranged." Michael leaned forward, his right hand raised to give an elegant flick that would turn his spoken word into reality.

"No need." Alex shook his head. "I like being in the trenches."

"Of course." Michael smiled and lightly clasped his hands on the surface of his desk. A maverick indeed. Most GAs preferred to rest between cases, taking a short vacation in one of the Heavenly spas and sports complexes. But not Alex. He might complain about the weather and the humans around him, but his heart and soul were tied to the occupants on that lump of rock and water called Earth. Commendable but it could also lead to burn out.

Alex had been in his employ for centuries and Michael felt he knew the angel inside and out. Which was why, when he sensed a subtle change in the man's demeanour, he'd taken pains to determine the cause and then find a potential treatment. Unfortunately, sometimes the cure was more dangerous than the ailment.

"I'm sure you didn't call me in today to discuss my living arrangements." Alex seemed to have tired of their idle conversation. Yet another cause for concern. The man never relaxed. "Do you have a new assignment for me?"

"Could there be any other reason I'd send for you?" Michael raised a brow and enjoyed watching the frown that flitted over the GA's face before his expression cleared. More than once, he'd had to call Alex on the carpet for his unorthodox approach to an assignment.

"Not that I can think of."

"Or at least not that you'll admit to," Michael murmured as he reached for a file of papers that were neatly stacked on the corner of his desk. He took a moment to flip through the pages, lips pursed, before handing it over to Alex's outstretched hand. "Her name is Emma."

"A girl?" Alex flicked the file open, barely glancing at the contents.

"A woman. She's twenty-seven."

"Occupation?"

"It's in the file, if you'd take the time to read it yourself." He chided the GA lightly before answering. "For the record, she's an accountant."

"Oh." A hint of disappointment tinged Alex's tones.

"Is that a problem?"

"No. Not really. I was just hoping for something a bit more exciting. Most of my cases have been pretty straightforward lately."

"Well," Michael made a show of furrowing his brow. "If this case doesn't suit you, I seem to recall there's a mall Santa who will be in need of a guardian angel. Someone to help him with all those children..." He let his voice trail off before fixing a hard stare on the man before him. "Would you be more interested in that job?"

"You're kidding, right?"

Keeping his expression bland, Michael secretly smiled. He possessed an excellent poker face and sometimes enjoyed watching the GAs try to second guess him. After a moment of studying him, Alex sighed, apparently not willing to call his bluff.

"No, thanks anyway." Alex made a face while rising to his feet. "On second thought, I'll stick with the accountant."

Michael nodded. "Excellent choice. She really does need you."

"What's the situation?" Alex paused, his hand on the door.

"She's scheduled to die."

Chapter 1

Emma pushed her grocery cart around the store one more time, slowing as she passed the produce section. Her cart contained all the items on her shopping list but she had a sudden yearning for something different. Something fresh and versatile. A poster caught her eye advertising the virtues of zucchini; grilled zucchini, julienned zucchini, zucchini baked with parmesan.

Zucchini?

She'd never purchased one before but... A glance towards the vegetable bins revealed it was on sale this week. She shrugged. Why not take a walk on the wild side?

Zucchini was wild? Chuckling to herself at the idea, she propelled her cart towards the display and reached for one of the oblong objects only to realize someone else had the same idea.

"Sorry," she apologized as her fingers brushed with those of a fellow shopper. Sparing a glance at the person beside her, she caught her breath. Standing beside her was the most gorgeous man she'd seen in ages. A wide smile, arresting grey eyes. There seemed to be a glow or an aura about him, something that pulled her towards him, creating a warm feeling around her heart. Unable to help herself, she tried to step closer.

"Oof." Something hit her in the stomach and she looked down, surprised to see she was leaning over the handle of her grocery cart. Heat flooded her cheeks. Crap. What must the man be thinking of her? Peeking up at him through her lashes, she saw he was looking at her, one corner of his mouth curved upwards. The glow she'd seen a moment earlier was gone; most likely a trick of the overhead fluorescent lighting. He was still incredibly good-looking, though.

She cleared her throat. "The zucchini is on sale this week."

"Yes, it is."

"I don't usually buy it. It was just an impulse."

"Really?"

Good heavens, she was babbling. "I'll...aah...just take this one." She grabbed a random vegetable, not looking at what was in her hand.

"That's not a zucchini." His eyes were twinkling now, a full-blown smile on his face.

"It's not?" Confused, she checked what she was holding and shook her head. She'd grabbed an eggplant instead. "Ugh! As first impressions go, this isn't stellar, is it?"

"I don't know." He leaned against a nearby pillar. "I've never met anyone over a zucchini before. Maybe this is how it's supposed to go."

She gave him a rueful smile. "I doubt it. I should have said something clever and witty."

"Witty and clever are over-rated. I like the down-to-earth, I-think-I'll-try-zucchini-today kind." He sounded so serious that she couldn't help but laugh.

"You're goofy."

"No, he's a cartoon character. My name's Alex."

Emma took his extended hand. "I'm Emma."

"Pleased to meet you." He held her fingers a second longer than necessary before letting them go.

"So..." She rocked on her feet, not sure what to say next.

"So..." He flicked a glance at her cart. "It looks like you're almost done with your shopping. Once you've checked out, would you like to go for a coffee?"

Emma hesitated, then nodded. She didn't know him but coffee in a public place was pretty safe. "Okay. There's a café just across the street. I could meet you there in ten minutes, if that gives you enough time."

"Sure. I'm only here to pick up a few things. See you soon."

Alex pushed his cart towards the bakery section of the store and Emma headed to the checkout. It was only as she was paying that she realized she'd completely forgotten to pick up a zucchini!

Alex busied himself looking at loaves of bread and packages of pastry while waiting the required time before meeting Emma. As a guardian angel, he had no need to buy groceries, let alone eat but, as part of his cover, he often found himself emulating humans. He picked up a container and pretended to read the label, all the while thinking about his meeting with Emma.

It had gone well. The subliminal messages he'd placed around the store had led her to the produce section just as he had planned. He'd arrived at the zucchini table at exactly the right moment and had charmed her into meeting him for a cup of coffee. The assignment should prove to be fairly straight forward...except for the fact that the woman was going to die.

He frowned, the knowledge not sitting comfortably with him. She seemed too young for such a fate. Oh, he knew people died at all ages but there was something about her that made it seem...wrong. Her self-deprecating smile, the hint of laugher that danced in her eyes; she seemed full of life. Maybe there'd been a mistake. A quick call to Michael might be in order. The archangel could double check his facts and... No. Michael didn't make that kind of mistake.

Sighing, Alex placed the package he'd been looking at back on the shelf. He'd have to accept the inevitable and do his best to support Emma during her final weeks of life. Would she be hit by a car? Come down with a rapidly advancing disease? He hoped she wouldn't suffer too much. Regret washed over him as he acknowledged he wouldn't be allowed to save her. He rubbed the back of his neck. Damn, this might very well be the hardest assignment he'd ever been sent on!

"Excuse me, sir."

Realizing he was blocking the aisle, Alex continued to push his cart through the store until it was time to meet Emma and then headed across the street to the coffee shop. She was already there; he could see her in a booth by the window. Pausing near the entryway, he studied her for a moment. She was watching a young mother with a baby in her arms and a toddler in tow. From the look on Emma's face it was obvious she loved children. It was a shame she'd not live long enough to become a mother.

His heart felt heavy at the thought and he had to paste a smile on his face before crossing the room to where Emma was waiting. As he slid into the seat opposite hers, a smile lit her face. She really was lovely.

"Hello again."

"Hi!"

She seemed more composed now and he gave an inward nod of satisfaction. His goal was to become her friend, not have her on edge around him. Michael would probably frown about that; the archangel often touted the importance of maintaining a certain level of detachment. Alex gave a mental shrug. Another stuffy rule. His gut was telling him Emma was going to need a friend and that's exactly what he planned to be. He'd deal with Michael when the time came.

"Would you like a coffee or…?" He nodded toward the counter where orders were placed.

"Hot chocolate, not coffee. And I want extra whipped cream."

He raised his brow and she held up a hand indicating he shouldn't talk.

"Don't judge me for hitting the chocolate so early in the day. Maybe I had a very trying week."

"Did you?"

"Well, no more so than normal."

A chuckle escaped him. "I know better than to get between a woman and her chocolate."

She propped her chin on her hand and grinned. "I knew there was a reason I liked you."

"I'll get our drinks and then you can tell me about your week."

They lingered over their beverages, Alex listening attentively as she explained the frustrations an accountant faced on a weekly basis, making her see the humorous side of unbalanced ledgers and missing receipts. When he suggested dinner, she readily agreed and they walked to a nearby restaurant. His taste in music and movies matched hers and they had a friendly debate over whether remakes were ever as good as the originals.

"You can't deny the special effects they use nowadays are superior to those from fifty years ago." Emma folded her napkin and sat back in her seat.

"But a good movie is more than special effects. They try to use explosions and camera tricks to distract you from what's really important, the plot and the acting." Alex punctuated his point with a wave of his fork before popping a final bite of pie into his mouth.

"Will there be anything else, sir?" The waiter paused by the table. "Coffee or liqueur?"

Alex gave her a questioning look and Emma shook her head. "I'm fine."

"Just the bill, then."

"Very good, sir." The waiter set the bill folder on the table and left.

They both reached for it at the same time. Their fingers brushed and Emma paused wondering if she imagined the delicious little tingle that seemed to race up her arm. She shook her head; they'd just met and she didn't put any faith in stories of instant attraction. Paying her fair share of the meal was what she needed to focus on. She gave the folder a gentle tug but Alex tightened his grip on it.

"My treat."

"No, you paid at the café."

"But I invited you."

Emma shook her head. "We've just met. A coffee is one thing but this is a whole meal. I should at least pay half."

"What if I told you I could write it off as a business expense?"

She cocked her head to the side. "Can you?"

He grinned. "Not really."

"Then I pay my share." She gave the folder a definite tug and Alex released it. After glancing at the total, she began to rummage in her purse. "So, what do you do for a living?

"It's…a form of personal security work."

"Like a policeman or a bodyguard?"

"It's complicated and very hush-hush. I really can't say much about it." He gave a shrug.

"Oh." She gave him a hard stare. "Nothing illegal, I hope."

He laughed. "I'm definitely operating on the right side of the law."

"Good."

After the bill had been dealt with, they left the restaurant only to pause outside. It was dark now, the street lights creating the illusion of a warm golden glow that seemed to counteract the chill in the air.

Emma stared up at the man who stood before her. It felt as if Alex had been made specifically for her. She couldn't think of a time she'd enjoyed an evening more and was loathe for it to end. But all good things had to end, right?

He was staring down at her, an unreadable look in his eyes. She took a deep breath, ready to end the evening.

"Would you like to go for a walk?"

His question surprised her and she opened her mouth to say no. They'd already spent hours together. She didn't know much about him. It was late and the streets were almost empty. She had to go to work tomorrow.

"All right." The words were uttered before she even realized it.

Alex tucked Emma's hand over his arm and they began to slowly stroll down the sidewalk. The air was crisp and cold but he didn't mind it for once. Emma's presence at his side seemed to warm him. It was a crazy notion, of course.

Her steps slowed and he realized she was fumbling in her pocket.

"Did you leave something at the restaurant?"

"No." She gestured with her head and a glance in that direction showed a woman standing beside a donation kettle. As they passed by, Emma dropped some money into the pot.

"Thank you." The woman beamed at her and Emma wished her a Merry Christmas.

"That was nice of you." He nodded in approval.

"I have so much; a home, a job, food. So many people are in need. I always keep some change in my pocket this time of year."

Generous as well as beautiful. A good sense of humour. Clever. The more he learned about Emma Campbell, the more he liked her.

He glanced down at her and she smiled up at him. Her hand tightened on his arm and he placed his hand over hers. A soft sigh escaped him. It felt right having her beside him. There didn't seem to be any need for words. Walking with her was enough.

Eventually, a park bench came into sight and of one accord they sat. A few snowflakes drifted down around them, landing in her hair and sparkling like diamonds. She tilted her face to the sky.

"It's a beautiful night, isn't it? Look at the stars. Have you ever wondered how many there are?"

"Not really."

"I have. I used to try to count them when I was a child. I guess I was always meant to be an accountant." She laughed softly. "Did you always feel drawn to your career?"

"Security? Yes. I guess so." He'd always been a guardian angel. It wasn't just a job. It was what he was. He couldn't even imagine doing anything else.

"I like to think that we're all put on this Earth for a specific reason; that we're here for a purpose. The trick is to find out what the purpose is and then do your best to fulfill it."

"I think you might be on to something."

"You do?" She turned to look at him. "You know, I want to be the best accountant I can be. I don't mean like being rich or becoming famous. I just want to…" She paused and seemed to search for words. "When I die, I want to leave the world a better place because I was in it. I want to make a positive impact." She gave a self-effacing laugh. "Exactly how an accountant is supposed to do that I have no idea."

"I don't know either, but I'm sure you'll find a way." He reached out to brush a wayward curl into place and his knuckles skimmed over her cheek. Her skin was smooth and cool from the winter air yet there was an underlying warmth, too. It went beyond physical body temperature. It shone from her eyes, showed in her smile. Slowly, he stroked his thumb over her cheek taking in each of her features.

Emma Campbell was something special. Beautiful on the outside but, more importantly, beautiful inside.

His eyes locked on hers and ever so slowly he leaned closer, gauging her response. When their lips were but a breath apart he paused, giving her time to protest and then closed the gap between them sharing a slow, sweet kiss.

That evening, Alex lay in his bed staring at the ceiling, thoughts of Emma swirling in his mind. Leaving her at her apartment door had been one of the hardest things he'd ever done. For some reason, he felt drawn to her, felt the need to stay close and it wasn't because of some danger lurking in the shadows. When he was with her, he felt…complete, as if some missing part of himself had been found.

It was ridiculous of course. Emma was a client. He was a guardian angel temporarily assigned to her. He didn't need her in his life. It was likely some weird aftereffect of their kiss.

He shifted position, the springs of the bed creaking faintly as he moved. The room seemed too warm and he shoved back the covers. What was the thermostat set at? He rolled out of bed and padded over to where the control unit was and adjusted the temperature.

Rather than returning to bed, he walked to the window and stared out at the cityscape. Most of the windows were dark, the residents sleeping. Somewhere out there Emma was sleeping, too. He pictured her in her bed, curls spilling over the pillow, a soft smile curving her lips. Was she thinking of him, of their kiss, like he was?

It had been soft and sweet and completely unplanned. Their lips had brushed gently once then twice before settling. It hadn't been long or deep yet the taste of her still lingered and he hungered for more. He leaned against the window frame, the coolness generating from the glass feeling good against his overheated flesh. With a sigh, he stared up at the night sky.

Damn.

He'd kissed a client.

Another rule broken.

Michael would *not* be happy.

Chapter 2

Alex cast a sidelong look at the woman beside him in the theatre. Emma Campbell still fascinated him. She might be an accountant but she was nothing like any stereotypical description he'd ever read. Her love of numbers and balanced books disappeared outside of work, leaving a fun-loving, vibrant woman. His gaze drifted over her features; make that a beautiful woman. A pert nose, full sexy lips.

He allowed his eyes to linger on her mouth, recalling the feel of it beneath his own, on his chest, trailing lower… His body responded to the memory and he shifted in his seat.

Her hand reached out to take his and he linked their fingers, giving a gentle squeeze. She flicked a glance at him with her expressive brown eyes, smiled and then returned her attention to the movie screen.

A shadow of regret passed over him. Theirs was not a normal relationship. How could it be? After all, he was her guardian angel except he wasn't supposed to guard her. She was scheduled to die and the knowledge didn't sit easily with him. He inwardly railed against that fact wishing there was a way to change the path of fate.

He'd even nipped into the office, catching Michael in the hallway, asking if there was a way events could be rearranged. Michael hadn't been in the least bit helpful basically telling him to do his job or hand in his halo. Alex had left, barely holding back the bitter words that had sprung to his lips. He'd always loved being a guardian angel yet now the conflicting feelings that plagued him were causing him to question all he believed in.

In the past, he'd been sent to guard and protect, to *save* people from danger, not to stand idly by waiting for them to die. Offering comfort and guidance as someone passed into the Heavenly realm was new for him. He was a man of action, dammit; figurative 'hand-holding' was new ground and he was feeling his way with this case more than ever before. A bit of guidance from Michael wasn't asking too much, was it?

With a soft sigh, he reflected on the past few weeks. He'd begun with the idea of making her last month on Earth as happy as possible, first arranging that simple meeting at the grocery store, then taking her on dates, striving to be the most entertaining companion she'd ever met. And, he paused and grimaced, somewhere along the line he'd gotten involved. Big problem. He was going to get raked over the proverbial coals when this was over.

Alex stroked his thumb over the back of Emma's hand. Delicate bones, yet strong. She liked to play the piano, was fond of flowers and animals, held the door for seniors, always dropped her spare change in the mission kettles that popped up at this time of year. The world needed more people like her. How could she be scheduled to die?

His stomach clenched at the thought, a heavy feeling settling in his chest. Changing fate wasn't one of his angelic abilities. Only the Big Guy could do that.

Emma's hand moved in his. She was standing up. With a jolt, he realized the movie was over. Just as the lights flicked on, he arranged his features into an appropriate expression once more becoming her oh so attentive boyfriend.

"Oh my gosh, that was the worst movie I've seen in, well, forever. It was so bad, it was funny." Emma leaned against Alex's side as they exited the theatre, enjoying the comforting feel of his arm wrapped around her. They'd been dating less than a month yet already it felt strange not to have physical contact with him. Who would have thought that two people reaching for the same zucchini in the grocery store could lead to something so perfect? And the funny thing was she never bought zucchini. The idea had just popped into her head! Now she'd always have a certain fondness for the vegetable; after all, it had led her to Alex!

"It *was* absolutely dreadful." Alex, not knowing the wayward path of her thoughts, continued to discuss the movie they'd just seen. "All the critics panned it." A smile played over his lips as he looked down at her.

She pulled away and smacked him lightly. "Then why did you suggest we see it? We could have stayed home and played cards or something."

"To take your mind off your problems." He grabbed her hand so she couldn't hit him again. "Now tell the truth; you didn't think about work even once during the movie, did you?"

"No." She made a face. "I was too busy trying to figure out the plot."

Alex leaned close and lowered his voice to a conspiratorial whisper. "Shhh, it's a secret but…" He paused and looked around to ensure no one was listening. "There wasn't one."

Emma burst out laughing and he hugged her close before putting his hand in the small of her back, urging her to follow him.

"Let's go this way."

"Why? We're parked over there." She pointed in the opposite direction.

"I know but I want you to see something."

"Not another bad movie. Please. My brain cells couldn't handle another attack."

"Trust me. You'll love this." Alex gave her arm a gentle tug and she followed, a happy bubble filling her heart.

Alex was so nice. Good-looking, witty, always ready for a new adventure. Brave. Insane! After all, who else but a crazy man would hang around a woman who'd been figuratively poking a stick in a hornet's nest? God, how had she ever gotten mixed up in such a mess? Being an accountant was supposed to be safe and boring. When she'd accepted a position at Stapleton, Royston and Collins and moved here, she'd anticipated a quiet nine-to-five job with weekends spent exploring her new city, making friends, perhaps meeting someone special… Well, the meeting someone special part had gone as planned but the quiet job was another story.

"Hey! No negative thoughts tonight, remember?"

Emma looked up to see Alex studying her, two vertical lines between his brows. "Sorry. I forgot."

He leaned down to kiss her forehead. "I'll let it go this once, but next time…"

"Next time what?" She gave him a cheeky grin.

"Next time, I might have to have my evil way with you." He wiggled his brows in what was probably supposed to be a menacing fashion.

She giggled at his efforts. "That's not a very scary threat."

"Hmmm…I forgot what a brave woman you are. I guess I'll have to think of something else then."

"I guess you will." She squeezed his hand and they walked in silence for a while, their breath appearing as little puffs, as she took in the sights and sounds.

The twenty-fifth was still a couple of weeks away but the weather was already picture perfect for a traditional white Christmas. Snow covered the ground; stars sparkled like diamonds in the night sky. The air was cold, nipping at noses and reddening cheeks.

The city was decorated for the festive season, too. Wreaths and bows adorned the lamp posts while stately pines sported strings of lights. Snatches of Christmas carols drifted from passing cars and late-night shoppers hurried along the sidewalks, arms loaded with packages.

Yes, Emma thought, it was a picture perfect night. Just like the man beside her. Dark blond hair with disorderly curls, clear grey eyes that twinkled with laughter. And his body…she gave a little shiver as she recalled the feel of it, hard against hers, the previous night.

Her lips curled into a smile as she recalled how they'd started the evening by making a simple meal together; pasta, salad, a bottle of wine. Then they'd begun to decorate her Christmas tree and had ended up tangled in tinsel, kissing under fake plastic mistletoe. How they'd ever made it to her bedroom, she still didn't know, but once they were there…

"What are you thinking?" Alex chose that moment to speak and when she glanced up at him there was a certain knowing look in his eye. She felt her face growing warm. There was no way he could know the direction her thoughts had been taking, and yet…

"Stop." He grabbed her shoulders and stepped in front of her.

"What?"

"Close your eyes."

"Why?"

He sighed. "Just trust me."

She hesitated and he prompted her further.

"There's something I want you to see. A surprise."

Giving in to his urgings, she complied. Eyes shut, she waited for his instructions.

"It's only a little ways away. Hang on to my arm. No peeking!"

Emma shuffled along at his side, surprised at how difficult it was to move about when you had to depend totally on someone else to guide you.

"You're doing fine. Remember, I'll always keep you safe."

The sound of his voice and the weight of his arm around her shoulders helped her relax. He'd always keep her safe. She liked the sound of the word *always*.

"Almost there. When I tell you to stop, I want you to count to ten and then open your eyes. Can you do that?"

She nodded and they walked a few more steps.

"Okay. Stop."

Following his instructions, she counted to ten before allowing her eyes to flutter open. A gasp escaped her. They were at the city park and a miniature Christmas village had been set up complete with tiny houses, decorated trees, snowmen, reindeer and Santa.

"It's adorable." She smiled up at him and he squeezed her shoulders.

"I knew you'd like it. They just finished setting it up today. Come on, we can walk through it." With his hand returning to its customary place in the small of her back, Alex led her through the streets. She laughed at the tiny train that chugged around the perimeter of the town, ooh'd and ahh'd at the mechanical Santa's workshop and marvelled at the stained-glass windows of the tiny church.

"This is my favourite part." Alex paused by a Nativity scene.

"Oh, look at the shepherds! And the angel." She pointed at a figure with a silver wire extending from its head and ending in a loop that roughly resembled a halo. Feathered wings tinged with pink stuck out from its back and slowly flapped in time to the music while it raised and lowered the candle clutched in its hands. Eyes raised to the heavens, its mouth was in a perfect 'O' shape.

Emma reached out and stroked the satiny robes edged with lace, then giggled at the glimpse of bare toes that peaked out from beneath the hem. "Isn't it adorable?"

"Do you really think angels look like that?" He gave her a sideways glance.

Emma shrugged. "I don't know. I *do* like Christmas angels better than chubby cupids and cherubs, though."

"Yeah, the cupid image…" Alex's voice trailed off and he made a face.

She gave a gentle laugh. "I bet you looked like a cherub when you were little. All those golden curls." Reaching up, she brushed his hair from his forehead.

Their gazes locked and the smile slowly left her face. The atmosphere between them changed.   Her breath quickened. She slowly trailed her hand around to his neck. A gentle tug had him leaning closer. "Alex, sometimes I feel like I've known you forever."

"Really?" He gathered her close, his head beginning to tilt to the side for a kiss. "I feel the same way. Emma, I—"

He froze, his expression drastically changing. Spinning around, he shoved her behind him. "Emma, get down!"

"Alex? What—"

A loud popping sound filled the air. Alex jerked and fell back, knocking Emma to the ground, a cry of surprise escaping him.

Somewhere, someone screamed. "Oh my God, he's got a gun!"

Shouting, yelling, squealing tires... A cacophony of noise filled the air, obscuring the carols that had, just moments ago, been such a seasonal backdrop to the fairy tale scene.

Dazed, Emma pushed against the weight that pressed down on her. Somehow she managed to move it, only to realize that it was Alex.

"Alex? Alex!" Frantically she called his name, horrified at the rapidly spreading stain that was marring his coat. Oh God, he'd been shot!

What to do? What to do? First-aid training finally kicked in and she pressed her hands to his chest trying to stem the blood flow.

"I need help! Please! Someone call 911!" She shouted the instruction over her shoulder.

"Police and ambulance are on the way." Someone spoke behind her. "Is he breathing?"

"I...I..." Her voice trembled. She looked at his face. It was so still. There was no flickering of his eyelids. No vapour rose from his parted lips. Could she feel the rise and fall of his chest?

"I'm a doctor. Move aside." Someone nudged her and she complied, crawling so she was beside Alex's head. She raised a hand and touched his cheek, leaving red streaks on his skin. Her fingers were stained with blood and she absent-mindedly wiped them on her coat, all the while thinking how cold he felt. Too cold.

"I'm sorry, ma'am, but your friend—"

She ignored the voice, somehow knowing what the man would say and wanting to block it out. "Alex? Alex, speak to me." She got to her knees and brushed his curls from his forehead. Shock had finally given way to tears. They blurred her vision and she blinked rapidly trying to focus on his beloved face. "Say something. Please!" Her voice broke on the last word.

"Ma'am." There was a touch on her back but she didn't respond to the implicit command. Instead she took hold of Alex's shoulders, giving them a shake. Panic grew inside her, making it hard to think clearly, causing her voice to rise, to become harsher. "Alex, you can't leave me. Alex? Alex!"

Alex didn't respond. A snowflake landed on his face. First one, then another and another.

Hands tugged at her shoulders. "Ma'am you need to move out of the way."

She tried to shrug them off but she was forced to her feet, pulled farther and farther from Alex. Darkness began to close in on her and she fought to keep it at bay even as her knees gave out and she stumbled to the ground.

"No. No!"

Her screams echoed through the Christmas village while the mechanical angel slowly waved its candle and sang about peace on Earth.

Chapter 3

Alex stood in the shower, letting the water beat down on him. Dying was a messy business. He washed the blood from his chest and then grabbed the shampoo, squirting a liberal amount into his palm. Emma's hands had been covered in his blood when she'd brushed the hair from his forehead. Now his curls were decidedly sticky.

His hands slowed as they worked in the lather. Emma had cried over him and he still felt guilty about it. He hated to see her cry, especially since he'd been the cause. True, it wasn't his fault that he'd 'died', in fact he'd saved her life, but that hadn't been foremost in her mind. She'd been grief-stricken and there had been nothing he could do about it. Once she thought he was dead, there could be no contact between them anymore.

Stupid rules. A combination of anger and regret filled him. His heart ached at the thought of never contacting her again. Even worse, she was still in danger and he wasn't there to help her. That bullet had been intended for her, he was sure of it, given Michael's pronouncement that she was scheduled to die. He scowled wondering how he could protect her because he certainly wasn't going to stand by and watch her die.

His conscience gave him a firm prick. Saving Emma was going against the divine plan and that was not something a GA would do. He clenched his fists, his thoughts racing as he tried to find a solution to this untenable situation. A heavy sigh escaped him. He'd figure something out. He had to!

The water was growing cold. He flicked it off and stepped out of the shower stall and, grabbing a towel off the rack, began to rub himself dry. On the floor, his ruined clothes lay in a pile. Even if the blood stains could be removed the bullet hole through his coat and shirt were irreparable. Thankfully he kept a spare set at work. After dumping the damaged clothing in the trash, he padded to his locker and pulled out jeans and a t-shirt from behind his formal robes. As he dressed, he continued to puzzle over how to save Emma while still staying true to the vows he took as a GA. One fact was becoming increasingly clear to him. He loved Emma Campbell and he couldn't stand by and watch her die. He slammed the locker door shut. To hell with what fate had planned for her!

Instantly, he regretted the curse and offered up an apology. Even without the expletive his sentiment remained the same.

"Hey Alex! Are you in here?" The door opened and a tall, dark-haired angel popped his head in. "Oh, good, you are. I've been looking all over for you."

"Zeke." Alex gave a brief nod of acknowledgement. Zeke was a guardian angel in training and from all reports more of a menace to his clients than a help. Rumour had it Michael was looking for someone with the patience of Job to take Zeke under their wing. So far, no one had volunteered.

"I heard you just came back from a big assignment." Zeke stared at him, a look of awe on his face. "You were gone for almost a month! It must be—"

"Was there a reason you were looking for me?" Alex interrupted.

"What? Oh. Yes." Zeke fumbled through his pockets and pulled out a piece of parchment. "Michael sent me to give this to you."

"Thanks." Alex took the paper and, when it appeared Zeke was going to stay, he raised a meaningful eyebrow and nodded towards the door. "You can go now."

"What? Oh, sure. Well, it's been great talking to you, Alex." Zeke backed out of the room, managed to catch his robe on the door knob and then, finally, disappeared down the hallway. Alex shook his head wondering why Zeke persisted in wearing formal robes while in Heaven. It wasn't like anyone else around him did. Maybe he hoped looking the part of an angel would improve his performance? Giving a shrug, Alex opened Michael's message. He read it twice before crumpling the paper into a ball and throwing it across the room.

Alex stared at his boss, his gut churning with hate—no, he wasn't allowed to feel that emotion; rule number twelve in the guardian angel handbook. By sheer force of will, he toned it down to active dislike. Yes, at this moment he actively *disliked* the supercilious bastard he now faced. And he knew he'd have to do penance later for even *thinking* the word bastard. However, Michael had no idea what it was like in the trenches, the split-second decisions that had to be faced, the emotional toll it took. The fellow sat behind that desk as if he were some CEO of a major international conglomerate.

Actually, in a way he was. Or at least one of the major stockholders. A quick glance around the room revealed everything you'd expect to see in the office of a high-powered individual. A bookshelf filled with leather-bound tomes, a small meeting area to the side, plush carpeting, a platinum pen set neatly aligned in the middle of a gleaming desk top, the requisite laptop sitting next to a day-planner and, of course, large plate glass windows that provided a million dollar view.

Yes, Michael fit the bill for a high-powered executive and, at that moment, Alex would like nothing better than to thumb his nose at the man and announce he'd quit rather than dance to the man's tune. He knew he couldn't though. The job was his life; bailing out wasn't an option.

"Do you have any idea how many rules you broke during the course of this assignment?" Michael glared at him across the polished surface of his desk.

Keeping his voice steady, Alex replied. "Yes, I know exactly how many and which rules I broke. It's always been my opinion, however, that any law can be broken in order to save a life. It's a creed I've followed throughout my career."

"'*To save a life*! Emma Campbell was scheduled to die. You took the bullet for her, potentially interfering with the divine plan."

"You never said *when* she was scheduled to die." Alex countered. "It could be from old age, couldn't it?"

Michael's usually passive face suffused with colour and Alex idly wondered if the deep rose tint was going to darken to purple. After a moment, the man seemed to regain some control, the colour subsiding though his tone was still accusing. "And you had sex with the woman the night before!"

"That's correct. I did." Alex narrowed his eyes and jutted his chin. He had no regret for any of his actions where Emma was concerned.

"Damn it, man, you're not supposed get that close to a client. What if she'd felt the skin flaps covering your wings? You'd have been exposed. We all would've been exposed."

The fact that Michael was angry enough to swear shook Alex for a moment but he quickly recovered. He leaned back in his chair and folded his arms. "There was no danger of exposure. I had a selective mind-wipe in operation. She thought she was making love with a human male." Yes, Alex thought, they'd made love. What had happened between them wasn't just sex. It had been two halves becoming a whole, a sharing of heart, mind and soul.

"A *selective* mind-wipe huh? She may not remember your wings but she definitely remembers you and some of the odd things that happened while you were around." Michael pulled open a drawer and withdrew a folder. "Do you know what this file contains?"

"I doubt it's a recipe for angel food cake." Alex eyed the file with mild curiosity. Michael always had reams of information about clients but seldom deigned to share it.

"Your attempt at humour is not only weak but ill-advised." Michael set the file down with a decisive thud, rose from his chair and walked around the desk only to lean back against the edge. "Now, not only is she still alive, she's mourning your death. And, she's been making some very inconvenient inquiries with the local police and hospitals. Seems she wants to bury you. We're sending in Zeke to clean up the mess you left and to continue your assignment."

"Zeke?" Alex rolled his eyes at the mention of the bumbling guardian angel wannabe. "He's completely incompetent."

Michael made a face. "I gave him a temporary power boost as he's the only man available. Christmas is our busy season, you know. A lot of humans find this time of year stressful."

"A power boost? Those only last for a few hours." Alex shook his head. "Zeke can't even protect himself let alone a human. You have to let me go back."

"No. Protecting her isn't the point. This GA assignment was solely to provide support and comfort until the scheduled event. And that will continue to be the mission. We did a global area wipe; no one involved in the incident remembers a thing. Zeke will go in, perform another complete mind-wipe on her as the first one obviously didn't take and then hover until her ultimate fate occurs."

He opened his mouth to protest and Michael shot him a warning look.

"I'm warning you, Alexander, keep your distance from Emma Campbell. Agree or you'll be confined to a very cold, distant cloud."

Alex slouched in his seat and gave the appearance of reluctantly agreeing. All he had to do was get through this interview and get out. Once free of Michael's meddling presence he'd head back to the human realm and plan his next move.

Chapter 4

Emma stared at the fire trying not to cry and failing miserably. She took deep breaths and blinked rapidly but her vision of the merrily dancing flames in front of her continued to blur. Her chin trembled with suppressed sobs, her throat and chest felt tight as she shredded the tissue in her hands.

Beyond the crackling of the fire, the small apartment was silent. No one hummed in the background as they made coffee or sighed as they settled onto the couch. She was alone; the comforting sounds she longed to hear were gone forever, just like Alex. In the corner of the room, the Christmas tree they'd decorated together twinkled brightly, its baubles and tinsel sad reminders of what she had lost. Part of her wanted to take the tree down, to block out all thoughts of the approaching holiday, while the other half of her wanted to cling to the memory of their last day together.

Oh what the hell, she thought leaning her head against the back of the chair, let the tears fall. Who was she trying to impress? Alex was dead and she felt like her heart had been ripped from her chest. The man she'd loved… No. That wasn't right. Had was past tense. She still loved him. He was gone but she'd never stop loving him. The pain might fade, eventually, but he'd always reside in a part of her heart, no matter what anyone else might think.

The doubting tones and pitying looks of the police played through her mind. When she'd contacted them today, they hadn't found any records to corroborate her story. No shooting. No listing for an Alex Flint residing in the city. They thought she was crazy, that she'd made the whole story up, but she knew differently no matter what they might say.

She clenched her fists and beat them rhythmically on her thighs in time with her thoughts.

He *had* been real.

He *had* existed.

The shooting *hadn't* been a dream.

The past few weeks weren't a figment of her imagination!

The man she loved was gone and she had every right to the pity party she was now wallowing in. A box of tissues, comfy old clothes, her hair a disaster. All that was missing was a tub of ice cream. Ice cream made her think of Alex. He'd loved the stuff. In fact, she still had a tub of his favourite flavour in her freezer. She'd likely never eat it, always keep it in the insane hope he'd return. She gave a weak laugh.

Insane. That was her. Mourning for a man no one believed existed.

She rubbed the moisture away from her eyes and pushed herself out of the armchair. Needing to do something, she moved over to her piano. Playing it always soothed her. Picking out a tune in a desultory manner, she realised she was playing the Christmas carol that the mechanical angel had been singing in the miniature village when Alex had been shot. She quickly pulled her hands away from the keys. Every detail from last night was vividly etched in her mind. Like a movie, it played over and over. The sound of the shot, the weight of Alex's body as he fell on her, the stark contrast of red blood against pure white snow. There was no way she could have imagined all of that. She turned on the piano stool, and stared at the phone. Maybe she should call the police and try to explain again.

No. They'd already told her they had no records and no witnesses to the shooting in the park. No hospital or morgue had received a body fitting Alex's description.

In fact, there was no evidence that an Alexander Flint ever existed.

After passing out in the park, she'd regained consciousness to find herself on her sofa with no recollection of how she'd got there. In fact, for a few minutes she thought she'd awoken from some strange dream but ticket stubs from the movie theatre and the blood stains on her coat had dispelled that idea. She knew she wasn't crazy, that her memories of the man were real. So why was everyone so sure she was hallucinating?

A sudden shiver shook her body and she walked over to the window to close the curtains. Her building was old and prone to drafts and creaks and doors that didn't shut properly. Some might complain, but for the most part she felt the high ceilings and decorative details more than made up for those minor inconveniences. Glancing down at the street below before she shut out the night she noticed the shadowy figure of a man. As big as Alex with a similar build but he appeared darker, more swarthy in colouring. He stood just at the edge of the pool of light thrown by the street lamp opposite her building. Frowning, she realized she'd seen him earlier in the day as well. He'd been at the newsstand where she'd bought a paper, hoping for a report of the shooting. Someone new in the neighbourhood? Or was he watching her?

That thought sent another shiver over her. Was he working for the Montrose corporation? Could he be the one behind the attack? The cops might say nothing had happened, that what she insisted was a gunshot had just been a car backfiring, but she knew differently. She was sure she'd been the intended target of that one lone bullet and Alex had died in her stead.

One bullet. One deadly accurate bullet that had left an innocent man bleeding to death in the snow. Alex was gone. She'd never see him again. Never hear his laughter or feel the warmth of his hand holding hers.

Tears welled in her eyes once more; an unbearable ache filled her chest. She wrapped her arms around her middle, trying to hug the memory of love to her body. Sinking to the floor, she rested her head against the wall and tried to understand what was happening. And why.

It'd all started about a month ago, just after she'd met Alex. She'd been going over the books for Montrose's chain of nightclubs. Inelegantly, she snorted; now, there was a misnomer! They were strip joints and rumours abounded that there were criminal connections as well. Perhaps that was why she'd taken extra care with Montrose's account or maybe it was just a coincidence that she noticed a discrepancy during the course of her monthly review of the ledgers. And, once she'd noticed it, she'd started to pull previous files and had begun to check back.

Then, just two days after she'd pulled the archived files she'd been called into the partners' conference room. Mr. Stapleton had been seated behind the expanse of the highly polished table while she'd sat in a single, straight-backed chair facing him. The look in his eyes had been cold and no hint of a smile had graced his face. He was a far cry from the paternal looking man who'd interviewed her for the job less than a year earlier. She had felt like she'd been called in front of the Spanish Inquisition.

"Ms. Campbell, it has come to our attention that your present caseload is taxing your abilities."

"Taxing my abilities?" Her eyebrows had shot upwards; her professional skills had never been questioned before.

"Yes. You've been putting in long hours to meet your deadlines. Your work is…satisfactory but…" He shook his head.

Satisfactory? Damned by faint praise. She'd opened her mouth to protest—just six months ago she'd been given a commendation for her handling of the Brisbane account— but wasn't given an opportunity to speak.

"However, we fear it isn't leaving you much leisure time. A case of all work and no play. We take the well-being of our clients and our employees seriously." The sharp look on his face had morphed into the fatherly look she was accustomed to seeing only there'd been a distinct air of insincerity about it. "An over-taxed employee makes mistakes, requires more sick leave, becomes dissatisfied which negatively impacts the morale of the whole company. With that in mind, we're moving you to the New Image account. It should be an excellent fit for you."

"New Image – the beauty salon chain? But what about Montrose Incorporated?"

"Ian Newcombe will take over that portfolio."

"Well…" She'd thought quickly, not wanting to lose all access to the Montrose files given her growing suspicions. "I'll be more than happy to help Ian with the Montrose account, at least until he's familiar with the books."

Mr. Stapleton had frowned at her suggestion. "We have the utmost faith in Ian's abilities."

"It's just…" She'd nervously licked her lips, feeling if she didn't speak up, she'd never have the opportunity again.

"Yes?"

"I…I've noticed a discrepancy in the Montrose files and I became curious about some of the entries. The numbers seem to balance, but when I checked back a few months—"

"Enough." Mr. Stapleton had leaned forward and hit the desk surface with his hand, the sound causing her to jump. "Ms. Campbell, I've been more than patient with you. It's obvious that even the bare basics of accounting escape you when dealing with a portfolio as large as Montrose. You've been given your new assignment. Confine yourself and your curiosity to New Image."

"But…"

His voice had deepened, took on a warning tone. "Stay away from the Montrose account. If you continue to poke around in places where you're not invited you may find it bad for your health."

She'd opened her mouth to protest but closed it when he'd narrowed his eyes at her. Something about the way he'd said 'bad for your health' sent a shiver down her spine.

"You are dismissed."

She'd risen from her seat and hurried from the room before Mr. Stapleton decided to fire her. If she was let go by the firm, how long would it be before she could find another position as good as this one?

Making her way back to her work station, the once friendly atmosphere of the firm had seemed absent. Those she'd passed in the hall hadn't met her gaze for as long as usual, the nods and smiles were cooler. And when she'd passed by the small coffee station, had the conversation paused and then continued on in quieter tones? Maybe it was all her imagination. Or maybe she'd been wearing rose-coloured glasses all these months. Surely everyone in the firm couldn't know she'd been subtly demoted for poking her nose into the Montrose account?

Back in her office, she'd pulled up the New Image file but her mind hadn't been on learning the ins and outs of a beauty salon. Thoughts of what she'd discovered kept swirling around in her head. What if her suspicions were true? What if Montrose's businesses weren't on the up and up?

She'd spent the next few weeks giving Ian Newcombe gentle prods and eventually not-so-subtle hints about there being problems with the books. The man had brushed her off, even going so far as to tell her he'd been informed that unpleasant things might happen to people who got too curious, and that he, for one, was just going to do what he was told. He rather wanted to keep his job. He'd raised an eyebrow and given her a meaningful stare. That had been two days before the shooting.

Pulling herself back to the present, she stood up, tugged the curtains shut and returned to her chair only to bounce back up to her feet. Dammit, was she going to sit next to the fire and mope or was she going to try and find out what the hell was going on? She was made of sterner stuff than this! Alex deserved better than one person mourning his death. He deserved justice; to have his death avenged by someone throwing his murderer behind bars. And, based on her conversations with the police, that someone would have to be her. She'd ferret out his killer and make the police listen to her! In her gut, she just knew this had to be related to the error she'd found in Montrose's books. She gave a decisive nod. Those books would be the logical place to begin her snooping.

Checking her watch, she saw it was almost midnight. Hmm… Perhaps she could put in some extra time on the salon chain's books. A long, lonely weekend stretched ahead of her so she might as well get some work done, right? At least that was the excuse she'd give if anyone asked what she was doing. And, while she was collecting her papers from the office, she might just copy some of Montrose's as well.

She smirked, feeling pleased with her plan. No one would be around at this time of night, especially on a Friday. Well, no one except the security guard, Mr. Morris, and he was a sweetie. He was often coming in to work just as she was leaving, his thermos of coffee and a newspaper tucked under his arm. He wouldn't give her any trouble.

Giving a nod, she reached for her coat only to pause. What about that guy downstairs watching her apartment? Emma turned out all the lights and eased the curtain away from the edge of the window. He'd gone! She pulled the curtain back completely and looked up and down the road outside. Nothing. Not a sign of him.

Someone watching her wasn't good but not knowing where that person had gone was even more unnerving. For a minute her imagination got the better of her. What if he'd entered the apartment building and was, at this very moment, standing in the hallway waiting to break down the door? Her heart started to pound and she hurried towards the door, intent on barricading herself inside when her more sensible self finally took over. There was a security lock on the building's entrances, front and back. It was the main reason she'd moved in to the place despite the steep rent. Most likely that man wasn't watching her at all. It was just a coincidence that she'd seen him twice today.

But you were shot at, the other half of her insisted. You need to be careful.

For a few moments she stood indecisively in the middle of the room before deciding to take action. She wasn't going to hide for the rest of her life but she'd take precautions. Risking her life after Alex gave his saving her hardly seemed a fitting way to repay him.

It only took a matter of minutes to change her clothes, stuff her long curls under a hat and to wrap a scarf around her face. Not a great disguise and it wouldn't stand up against close scrutiny, but the best she could come up with on the spur of the moment. Turning up her collar, she headed for the door.

Chapter 5

Alex hovered between his world and the human one, his wings barely moving. It was a neat trick and not one a lot of guardians could accomplish. He shook his head. Zeke certainly couldn't. Zeke might want to be a GA but he had a long way to go. The man wasn't even aware that another GA was in the area. Hell, Zeke was barely aware that *Emma* was in the area! As a matter of fact, she'd just passed his hiding spot in an alley and the man hadn't even blinked.

Shaking his head, Alex followed Emma's car. Zeke could watch the empty apartment.

Emma drove carefully through the nearly deserted streets, slush hissing under her tires. At this late hour only a few Christmas trees remained lit, solitary sentinels proclaiming the approaching holiday. The effect was lonely and forsaken rather than cheery. Through the rear window he could see Emma reaching up to brush her cheek as if wiping away a tear. His heart ached for her. She'd proclaimed to love Christmas but there was little room for joy in her heart right now. He sighed, the feeling of uselessness that had plagued him all day continuing to grow within him.

It had started when he'd visited Emma that afternoon. She hadn't been aware of his presence, of course. He'd remained invisible, helplessly watching her cry. It had taken every ounce of his willpower to stop himself from materializing in her living room.

He'd wanted to take her into his arms and kiss her tears away, but he couldn't. In her mind, he was dead and that was how he'd have to remain. Instead, he'd had to content himself with projecting the thought into her mind that whatever happened she would be safe. Right.

Emma Campbell is scheduled to die. Michael's words played in his mind and he shook his head unable to wrap his mind around that fact. What good could her loss do? Yes, he knew there was an ultimate plan, one bigger than even a GA could begin to comprehend, but it still seemed wrong that the good should die while evil flourished.

He made a face. Interfering with the Big Guy's plans just wasn't done and yet that was the course of action he'd taken, would continue to take. There'd be consequences, naturally, but he was willing to face them. Emma deserved to live a long, happy life. Oh, he'd keep his distance, just as he said he would but somehow he'd manage to keep her safe, at least until the whole shooting incident was cleared up. That was a satisfactory compromise wasn't it? He cast a look upwards and when no bolt of lightning incinerated him on the spot, he decided that was as good as an agreement.

She was turning into the parking lot behind her office building and he frowned. The area was dark, several of the street lights had burned out. Not a safe place for her to park. He quickly fixed them, getting the lights to flicker a few times before shining steadily. Emma frowned and looked around before shrugging and he gave a sigh of relief that she wasn't suspicious about the lights.

The parking lot was almost empty, only a few vehicles remained at this late hour. They likely belonged to the night time security guard and cleaning crew. Emma barely gave them a passing glance, her eyes fixed on the door, her stride determined. As she passed by, he admired the gentle sway of her hips and the length of legs showcased in tight jeans and knee-high boots. A few flakes of snow drifted down, clinging to her long lashes and melting on her very kissable full lips.

Unable to resist the temptation, he brushed his mouth over hers then cursed himself when she frowned and looked around, a puzzled expression on her face. Had she felt him? Sensed him? No, it shouldn't be possible.

He watched as she pressed her fingers to her lips. Her eyes grew distant as if she were lost in thought and then she gave herself a shake. Digging into her purse, she drew out her keycard and used it to enter the building. Alex drifted through the doorway after her, unabashedly listening in as she talked to the security guard.

"Ms. Campbell, what are you doing here? It's the middle of the night!" The grey-haired security guard set down the newspaper he'd been reading.

"Hello, Mr. Morris. I'm just collecting a few files. I couldn't sleep so I thought I'd put in some extra hours on a new account I was given."

"Paperwork on the weekend?" The man shook his head. "Time was a pretty little girl like you would be spending the weekend with her young man."

"I'm a career woman, Mr. Morris." Emma answered him airily as she jabbed the elevator button. Alex noticed how she compressed her lips and blinked against the sheen of tears that had appeared in her eyes.

Don't weep for me, sweet Emma. He whispered the words, wishing she could hear him.

"Well, don't work too hard. Take some time to enjoy yourself."

"I'll try, Mr. Morris." The elevator door swept open and Emma stepped inside. The security guard jotted Emma's name down in a log book and noted the time before picking up his newspaper and immersing himself, once again, in the sports scores.

Alex scanned the log; only the cleaning crew were in the building. Emma shouldn't run into any problems here but, just in case...

A single flap of his wings was enough to propel him upward. Effortlessly, he passed through the layers of steel and concrete, arriving in the accounting firm where Emma worked just as the elevator doors slid open.

Emma hurried towards her cubicle, the sound of her footsteps echoing down the empty hallways. Evening security lighting lit her way, glimmering off the few pathetic bows and bits of tinsel that hung here and there in a passing nod to the approaching holiday. The office areas off the hallway were mostly in darkness, cabinets and cubicle walls casting shadows that transformed the familiar into the realm of fear. Alex could sense how Emma's heart rate was escalating as she, no doubt, imagined bogeymen lurking behind every desk and filing cabinet.

Don't worry. There's no danger here. I'll always keep you safe. Once again, he breathed the reassurance into her ear and noticed how the tension in her shoulders seemed to ease.

She quickly collected a bunch of files from her cubicle and then went to another work station. Alex manoeuvred around so he could read the nameplate on the desk.

Ian Newcombe?

Ah, the person who had taken over the Montrose account. She'd mentioned the man to him. An ass kisser. Not that Emma had used the term but based on what she'd said, Alex had easily drawn that conclusion.

Emma searched the man's desk and filing cabinet before finding what she'd obviously been looking for. The name Montrose was clearly marked on the file. He knew she'd thought there was something fishy about the account and suspected she'd been pulled off it because of her suspicions.

"Emma, what are you doing?" He murmured to himself. "You said you were told to stay away from the account. What kind of trouble are you getting yourself into?"

Damn, he wished he had a magic mirror that could see into the future. GAs were only given information on a need to know basis and the future was strictly off-limits except in the most dire of circumstances. The fact that he'd been told Emma had been scheduled to die was a huge revelation on Michael's part, though necessary given the role he was supposed to have taken. In Michael's eyes he'd no doubt botched that part of the job. Too bad. Unfortunately, even though he'd saved Emma, he was still in the dark as to what was to come. Was she going to die regardless of his efforts? Or, by intercepting that bullet had he cheated fate and ensured her a long life?

"Humans have free will." Michael would drone during monthly squadron meetings. "We might believe we have their future completely mapped out, but at the last minute they could make a different choice and…" He'd wave his hands and shrug. "All I can tell you—all I know for certain—is that when you are on the job, the potential for danger exists from some quarter in your assignment's life. It could be an out of control truck, a freak storm, a criminal act or even a chicken bone stuck in the person's throat."

Grumbles were met with raised brows and an admonishment from the stuffy archangel. "Do your job. Stay alert. Be on guard. You *are* guardian angels, after all."

Yeah, Alex grumbled to himself. Stay alert. Be on guard. When was the last time Michael had been out in the field? The archangel had no idea what it was like to be on guard around the clock, seven days a week. Alex absentmindedly rubbed his chest. And when had Michael ever been shot? That had hurt. A lot!

Emma was making her way to the photocopier. He watched with a furrowed brow as she fed the papers through the machine before putting everything back where she'd found them. Damn, she even wiped off the handle of the filing cabinet to remove her fingerprints! Alex wasn't sure whether he should be proud of her or wring her neck for delving deeper into what might well be a dangerous situation.

She slipped the copies she'd made into a file folder and took a deep breath before tucking it under her arm. With a searching look around the workstation, she headed to the elevator.

"Find what you need?" The security guard smiled at Emma as she crossed the lobby.

"Yes, I did." She held up the file.

"Fine then. Have a good night and be careful how you drive." The guard glanced at his watch and then made a note in his log book.

"You, too, Mr. Morris." Emma breezed out of the building as if she didn't have a care in the world. Alex, however, could sense the adrenaline rush she was experiencing. The little minx was enjoying dipping her toes in murky waters!

Alex watched as she crossed the parking lot and got into her car. Once he heard the doors lock, he slipped back into the office building. The security guard was reading the newspaper again.

Perfect.

In the blink of an eye, Alex erased the log entries pertaining to Emma's comings and goings followed by a mind-wipe of the security guard before dashing into the parking lot in time to see Emma pulling out onto the street.

He made sure she arrived home safely before returning to the office. Finally he could be of some use to her; he needed to finish covering her tracks. Whatever she'd copied obviously hadn't been her work and he didn't want her to further endanger her life, if this was indeed where the danger might be coming from. It took only seconds to delete the copier's memory and alter the security camera recording. Emma had taken care of any fingerprints. Yep, he thought as he looked around, there was no evidence she'd ever been there.

By the time he arrived back at her apartment, Emma was asleep. For a moment he stood there watching her sleep. Her lashes were spikey, evidence that she'd been crying, and her hands were curled into fists as if prepared to fight some unknown foe. A heavy sigh escaped him. How he wished he could make everything right for her but it was beyond his powers. Reaching out, he brushed a long dark curl from her cheek.

Sleep well, my love. I'm here to guard you.

He willed the thought into her mind and then watched a smile sweep over her lips as she visibly relaxed and snuggled deeper into her pillow. If only he dared join her in the bed, hold her in his arms as she slept. But no, he needed to keep his distance. Instead, he'd occupy himself by looking through the papers she'd photocopied.

The files were all relevant to the Montrose account, but try as he might he couldn't see any discrepancies, nor could he see anything that looked like illegal dealings. He stared across the room, his mind racing. Why had she been warned to stay away from the account? And why had she been shot at? Had it been a random shooting, or a hired *hit* to keep her from digging deeper? Or perhaps the shooter had been paid to scare her off. What secrets did those numbers hide?

He needed to check out Peter Montrose, to see exactly what sort of dealings the man was involved in. Pulling out the desk chair, he settled himself down at her computer and logged into the private Heavenly search engines. If there was any information worth knowing about Montrose, it would be in the Big Guy's files.

Chapter 6

Emma stretched and slowly opened her eyes. The pillow cradled her head, the sheets gently stroking her skin as she moved. She felt more rested today; more than she felt she had a right to be. But she'd dreamed that Alex had been with her all night. It was only her subconscious playing tricks, but it comforted her to think that he was watching over her from whatever afterlife he'd entered.

Throwing back the covers, she got out of bed and made her way to the bathroom to shower and dress. This morning, she didn't choose comfortable old sweats. She had a sense of purpose about her and was ready for action.

After making some tea and toast, she sat down near the fireplace and began to flip through the Montrose files, making notes on anything that struck her as unusual.

Time crept by, her cup of tea grew cold, but the pages of notes grew longer and longer. By the time she was done, her hand hurt from gripping her pen and there was a definite crick in her neck. The physical discomfort was worth it though. She had a clearer idea, more or less, of what was going on plus a pile of evidence to support her claim…if her reasoning was correct.

Standing up, she arched her back and ran her hands through her hair. She wished she had someone to talk to. Someone she could bounce ideas off. That was one of the things she'd liked best about Alex. He'd been a great listener.

"I miss you, Alex. If you were here, you'd help me figure this out." She picked up her cold tea and walked to the sink to dump it down the drain, then refilled the kettle with water and put it on the stove to heat. "You know, if you don't mind, I'm going to use you as a sounding board."

It was silly of her to be talking to Alex as if he were there but a feeling of warmth surrounded her as she did so. The logical part of her said that most likely it was heat coming off the burner, but her heart would have her believe that somehow Alex was listening.

Grabbing an apple, she began to explain her findings to her dead lover.

"The Montrose books are balanced, except for the fact that a number of pay cheques have never been cashed. In a large business, there's always the odd case of a cheque that disappears in the mail but this is more than an occasional occurrence."

She took a bite of apple and chewed thoughtfully.

"I've written down the names of the employees that have never cashed their cheques. They're all females working at various nightclubs across the country. It would seem to me that none of these women have a large enough salary that they could afford not to cash their cheques. And if they'd simply misplaced them, why not go to the manager of the club and explain what happened? The original cheques could have been cancelled and new ones issued."

Emma paced the apartment as she finished her apple, trying to think of logical explanations for the uncashed cheques but not coming up with any ideas.

"You know what I think I need to do, Alex?" She made a fresh cup of tea as she spoke. "I need to do a web search on the names I wrote down. Maybe there's some connection between the women. They're from different parts of the country, but you never know." She sat down at her desk, logged on to the computer and began to search.

~~~

The archangel Michael looked like he was going to blow a gasket. Alex had never seen him so angry. For once his superior looked dishevelled instead of his usual suave self. His typical sharp suit had been replaced by t-shirt and jeans
~~~

and there was a distinct shadow of stubble covering the man's jaw line.

"Alexander, in all my days I have never, I repeat, never had to deal with such a recalcitrant guardian angel as you." Michael stopped his pacing and pinned him with a furious look. "Do I have to send you to appear before the Boss?"

For all his righteous indignation about being yelled at by Michael, Alex couldn't help but blanch at the thought of having to report to the Big Guy.

"He doesn't have to be involved in this, does he, Michael? It's not like I broke every one of the three thousand, eight hundred and twenty-two rules in the handbook." Alex hoped that a bit of levity would help the man see reason.

Referencing the absurd amount of red-tape that controlled a guardian angel's actions didn't have the desired effect. Michael scowled as, too late, Alex remembered the man facing him had co-authored the handbook.

"Unfortunately He's already involved. He was the one who called me in on my day off specifically to deal with you."

That explained the t-shirt and jeans, Alex mused.

"You deliberately went against orders and made contact with the client." Michael had begun pacing again. The furniture miraculously moved out of his way as he walked, yet another sign of how upset he was. The archangel wasn't given to theatrical shows of power. "You already interfered with the planned order of events. You were told you were off the case. What part of 'stay away from her' didn't you understand?" Michael stopped and sat down, his desk sliding into place in front of him. "Well? What do you have to say for yourself?"

"I didn't make actual contact. I merely checked up on her. Do we know why she was targeted and by whom? Does it have to do with Montrose Incorporated?"

"Don't try to soft-soap the situation. You *did* make contact. She sensed you were there."

It was no surprise that Michael knew he'd seen Emma last night; the archangel had spies everywhere! And, even if it wasn't a matter of spying, Michael had power to divine when a human began to notice their guardian angel. Exactly how and why Emma had sensed him was puzzling though. And really, her reaction had been too fleeting to be classified as an actual awareness.

"As to why she's been targeted," the archangel continued, "yes, *we* know. You, however, are all too familiar with the rules. Need to know basis only—and you don't need to know. 'Free will of humankind' and all that." Michael waved his hand signifying that detail was of no importance. "The important point here is that you didn't follow protocol while on the Campbell assignment, hence you were removed. You have no business being anywhere near her now."

Alex leaned forward, knowing he had to find some way to convince Michael that he had to stay involved. He might not know exactly what was going on but every guardian angel instinct he had was telling him his presence in Emma's life was vital. "She left her apartment late last night, did you know that?"

Michael raised his brows so Alex knew this was new information for his superior. Ha! So the man's spies weren't infallible after all. It gave him confidence enough to lean back in his chair and smirk. "No, I didn't think you'd heard. Zeke didn't even notice her when she drove right past him; the fellow is totally incompetent." He shifted in his chair, trying to remain relaxed and keep the edge of desperation from his voice. Cool logic was what Michael responded to, not impassioned pleading. "Don't you see? I have to go back on duty. If we leave Zeke in charge of her, she's basically facing her fate alone."

Michael sat in silent contemplation for some minutes. Curiously, Alex watched him, while fighting to keep his calm façade in place. There was a rumour that the archangels could communicate telepathically amongst themselves and with the Boss. His gut was telling him that such a communication was happening right before his eyes.

His assumptions were soon proven correct when Michael began to speak again. "You would have to agree to certain conditions before we could allow you to go back on duty."

"What conditions?" Alex asked warily.

"You must agree to abide by the rules."

He snorted. "The GA handbook—"

"Not those." Michael cut him off. "You've already proven that the normal rules aren't enough to curb your actions, therefore more stringent controls will be placed on you."

"Such as?"

"Agree first, then you will be informed as to what they are."

Dammit, they were purposely trying to scare him off the case! Anger filled him, but he wasn't going to succumb to their tactics. He needed Heaven's power in order to help Emma. She was all that mattered to him now.

Alex gave a small nod of agreement. "I agree to any and all conditions you deem fit to impose upon me."

"So noted." The archangel leaned forward, placed his elbows on the desk in front of him and steepled his fingers. "You will not touch or speak to Emma Campbell. Each time you disobey this command you will lose some of your immortality." Michael paused and gave him a warning look. "Do not think that this will eventually make you mortal or human. In actuality, what will happen is that with each contact you will gradually become more visible to the human world but only as a shade."

"A shade?" Alex frowned. "I'm not familiar with that term."

"Not surprising. Few guardian angels are reckless enough to warrant such a control being imposed on them. If you become a shade, it's irreversible. You are ghost-like to a human. Eventually, sufficient contact will render a shade corporeal."

"I'd have a human body?" Alex sat up straight, possibilities springing to his mind. He'd be able to be part of the human world. To live, love, possibly even marry and maybe even have children…with Emma. A smile began to creep over his face.

"Before you start to celebrate, Alexander, there is more. Yes, you will have a human body, but you will only be able to remain corporeal for twenty-four hours."

Not good, Alex thought, his grin fading. "Why only twenty-four hours?"

"The human body is frail relative to ours. It's an incredible strain on the autonomic nervous system to suddenly become a fully-grown adult."

"So, what happens after the twenty-four hours are up?"

Michael lifted an eyebrow. "You will simply cease to exist."

Ah. Definitely not good. He frowned as the severity of the situation began to sink in. As a guardian angel, his own life—and death—had never been an issue before, but now… He compressed his lips. He'd already agreed to the terms and was bound by them. Emma was worth the risk. Giving a nod, he spoke. "I understand, Michael. Thanks for the chance you're giving me." A thought popped into his head. "What about Zeke?"

"He will remain on the case as your assistant should you need him."

He opened his mouth to protest but Michael raised a warning brow.

"Consider yourself his mentor if it makes you feel better. Zeke's young; he has potential, if given a *proper* example to follow." Michael's voice trailed off as he levelled a meaningful look across the expanse of the desk.

Alex sighed. "Fine. He can be my back-up." Mentally he added 'when Hell freezes over'. Getting to his feet, he continued out loud. "Am I free to go now? I need to get back to Emma."

Michael stood up and came around his desk. "Alexander…" He paused and frowned, then started again. "Alex…I was young once myself, I'm sure you find that hard to believe, but it's true. I haven't completely forgotten the rush one gets when you save a life." A distant look came over him before he blinked and cleared his throat. Making direct eye contact, he extended his hand—an unheard of act from an archangel. "Be careful. We need competent and caring guardians like you."

Alex shook Michael's hand. The moment their palms touched he felt heat rush up his arm and spread through his body. What was that all about? Part of becoming a shade or some sort of warning? He wouldn't give Michael the satisfaction of asking though.

Letting go, he surreptitiously wiggled his fingers to rid them of the strange sensation and turned towards the exit. The door swung open as he approached; Michael was still showing the extent of his power. Alex stopped on the threshold and looked over his shoulder at his superior. "I'm not some rookie GA. I can do my job and be careful at the same time."

"I hope so, Alex. I really hope so."

Chapter 7

Emma pressed her hand to her stomach as if the gesture could somehow calm the queasy feeling stirring within her. Good heavens, what had she stumbled upon?

The results of her internet search were on the screen before her. All of the uncashed pay cheques had belonged to women who had been reported as missing by family or friends. She wondered if the police had discovered the relationship between the cases. As far as she knew, there'd been no items about it on the news. Perhaps, since the cases were scattered across the country, no one had yet made the connection.

Worrying her lip, Emma debated calling the police to share her discovery. Would they even listen to her though? After all, they all thought she was crazy for insisting 'a non-existent' Alex had been shot. More likely they'd write her off as some flake looking for attention by fabricating yet another story. Or…another thought crossed her mind…maybe there was some kind of cover-up going on. Montrose was rich. Perhaps rich enough to buy off certain law enforcement authorities?

Damn. She let her hand fall from the phone and began to pace the room using Alex as her sounding-board once again.

"You know, Alex, this could be coincidental. Not likely, but it could be. Sadly, women go missing all the time, especially those that work at establishments like Montrose's. Exotic dancing, drinking, possibly some illegal backroom gambling or drugs." She ticked the points off on her fingers then frowned. "It's all speculation though. What I need is proof. A reason behind the disappearances, some hint of wrong-doing on Montrose's part."

Of course, Alex didn't reply but she still felt better for having voiced her concerns to him. Besides, lots of people believed that the dead were still around in spirit. Emma clung to that belief right now, even though she'd never been a big proponent of it before. Alex had been too good, too kind, for his spirit to just disappear like that. No, she was sure he still existed on some plane. Now, if only he could tell her what exactly she'd discovered.

Uncashed cheques.

Women missing.

All worked at Montrose's clubs.

But why had they gone missing?

Emma sat down to scour over the files she'd copied once again. Was there a pattern? A certain day of the week or…? She trailed her finger down the column of numbers, flipped a page then paused and flipped back. This could be it! She arranged the pages so she could view them all at once and then double checked against the dates the women had been reported missing.

There it was! A substantial deposit from Seraphim Employment was made within a week of each woman going missing. And, interestingly enough, those were the only times that Seraphim Employment appeared in the books. The question now was what kind of a company was Seraphim Employment? A quick search of the internet told her that it was, on the surface, a legitimate employment agency, but perhaps there was another layer below the surface. After all, why would an employment agency pay Montrose? Surely it should be the other way around if the clubs were hiring from Seraphim?

Was Seraphim a front for something else? And if so, what? A nasty suspicion came to mind and she began to nibble on her fingernail, only to realize what she was doing and grimace. She thought she'd broken that habit!

"You know, Alex, this makes me think of that movie we watched a few weeks ago, the one about human trafficking. People disappearing without a trace, large sums of money involved." She shivered recalling the fate of some of the abductees. "Is that what's going on here? It could be. It would make sense but...I still have no real proof."

She sighed heavily. Who was she trying to fool? She wasn't some super-sleuth.

"Alex, if you were still here with me, I bet we could figure this out, they say two heads are better than one. Right now my head is drawing a blank." Emma plopped down on her desk chair and stared at her computer screen in the vain hope that it would tell her what to do.

Of course, it didn't. Idly, she navigated onto the website of her local newspaper. She read the headlines, scanned articles without really consciously registering what she was reading. As she was scrolling through the site a flashing ad on the side of the screen caught her attention. The Dusky Rose club was looking for wait staff.

Hey! She sat up straighter. All of Montrose's clubs had the word 'Rose' in their names. She reached over to the papers she'd purloined from Ian Newcombe's files and flicked through them until she came to the one with a list of Montrose's businesses. Sure enough the Dusky Rose was one of his clubs. And the ad said to apply to Seraphim Employment. That was the name of the random company that had appeared on the ledgers.

A smile began to curl her lips as an idea formed in her mind. She'd had a part-time job waiting on tables while at college so she had experience. And, if she was working right inside one of Montrose's businesses, she might be able to find some hard evidence to support her claim.

Did she dare apply for a job?

A voice inside her seemed to be yelling 'no' and pointing out all the possible pitfalls of going into enemy territory but she ignored it. She could ask for a week's leave of absence from work; Stapleton would likely be pleased if she wasn't around…

Yeah, why not?

~~~

What the hell was going on?

Against his better judgement, Alex had used Zeke to watch Emma while he'd been checking out Montrose. The young guardian had listed a non-eventful couple of days. The only notable event had been meeting someone at a café – a woman in a business suit – before going to the office yesterday. Then today, she'd gone shopping for clothes. It all seemed innocuous enough but there had to have been more to it than Zeke had reported.

For one thing, her purchases were completely out of character. He stared at the bed strewn with shopping bags and price tags. Whatever had possessed her to visit a sexy clothing store? Alex raked his fingers through his hair and stared in disbelief at Emma's garb as it disappeared beneath the coat she was donning.

Miniscule boy shorts and a sheer white blouse, if that tiny slip of material could be given such a grandiose name. And the top was tied together under her breasts, holding them like a bra. Which was good because it was obvious she wasn't wearing that part of her underwear. In fact, Alex moved to view her from behind, he was pretty sure she wasn't wearing any panties either; shorts that tight should have shown a panty line.

Perhaps he ought to have checked up on her before now, but he'd been busy watching Peter Montrose. Since it was obvious Emma wasn't going to abandon the hunch she had, learning as much as he could about the enemy had seemed a good idea. Unfortunately, after spending some time following the man to work and then back home again, he hadn't managed to garner much new information. That Montrose was both rich and powerful were established facts and the large entourage of staff had made sense given the size
~~~

of his estate and business holdings. The man's lunch, a weird combination of anchovy pizza and French champagne, had been curious but hardly useful. His wardrobe was filled with silk suits and designer labels while his movie collection ranged from action to porno to classics. It had been interesting to note, however, that he appeared to be a control freak, demanding every decision pass by him first. And, from the way he talked to his employees, he possessed a mean-streak; more than one person had visibly quivered when Montrose had expressed his displeasure over some minor event.

Alex shelved his musings when he saw Emma grab her handbag. He followed her out of the building and settled into the passenger seat of her car, studying her quizzically as she pulled out of the parking lot and drove downtown. His unease grew when she bypassed the brightly lit entertainment area and manoeuvred her vehicle into the part of town once known as the red light district. The prostitutes had long since been moved off the streets but the bars and clubs were barely disguised brothels. Nearly all of them had upstairs rooms which could be rented by the hour and high-stake poker games were rumoured to take place in private backrooms.

Emma pulled over to the side of the road and parked. She sat behind the wheel taking big gulps of air. Waves of nervousness and fear flowed from her body making Alex want to gather her into his arms. Mindful of Michael's warnings he didn't touch her. He was, however, going to stick extremely close to her.

She climbed out of the car, crossed the road and entered an alley, holding her bag as if it were a shield in front of her body. He pulled up the hood of his sweatshirt as he began to tail her then scoffed at himself over the pointless act. She couldn't see him. Giving his head a shake, he continued on.

The alley was typical in its graffiti-based decor, the damp walls dimly glistening in the faint lighting. There was a stench to the air; garbage, cooking grease, booze and urine; the dark corners had obviously served a double purpose as a latrine. Emma wrinkled her nose as she carefully stepped along, trying to avoid the dirty, slushy puddles that covered the ground. A pathetically malnourished cat yowled and darted out in front of her causing her to gasp. She jumped aside and bumped into a trash bin. The few bits of snow that had bravely remained atop the metal surface fell to the ground.

"Prophetic," Alex murmured to himself as he watched the white purity of the snow quickly swallowed by the filth below.

Emma, recovering from her fright, straightened and hurried on her way, finally stopping in front of a door with a single naked bulb hanging over the frame. Faded lettering on the panel proclaimed it was the employees' entrance for the Dusky Rose.

The club's name rang a bell; he remembered it from the list of companies and clubs owned by Peter Montrose.

It would seem his darling was doing some undercover investigative work. He shook his head. If anyone needed a guardian angel, it was Emma Campbell!

Chapter 8

"You the new girl?" The six-foot-six wall of ugly muscle addressed Emma as she stood in a narrow hallway just inside the rear of the Dusky Rose.

"Umm…yeah. I start this evening." She glanced around. "Ms. Martinez, the woman who offered me the job, said someone would show me the ropes. A girl named Marcie?"

'Wall' gestured for her to follow and led her to a small room lined with lockers. Two benches were arranged in the middle of the space. An old sink was mounted on a wall that needed repainting and topped with a cracked mirror. Emma inwardly frowned. For an organization as successful as Montrose, she'd have thought the establishments would be better maintained. Of course, the Dusky Rose wasn't exactly up-scale compared to some of the other holdings.

"Wait here," the man pointed at one of the benches. "I'll find Marcie and send her back."

Her legs felt like they'd turned to water and she collapsed onto the wooden surface, taking slow measured breaths to calm her rapid heartbeat. For the hundredth time she wished Alex was there, helping her solve this mystery she'd stumbled upon. She closed her eyes and pictured him as he'd looked when they were walking around the miniature Christmas village on that last night. Try as she might she couldn't keep his image steady. It kept changing and for some strange reason he was wearing a hoodie. That was odd. She'd never seen him wearing such a thing; why would she picture him like that now?

The clicking of high heels made Emma snap open her eyes. She turned to see a red-haired woman standing in the doorway.

"You Emily?" The unfamiliar name gave Emma a start until she recalled it was the pseudonym she'd chosen. She replied with a nod.

"Yes, that's me."

"My name's Marcie." She pointed to a locker. "This one is yours. Put your coat and bag in it and make sure you leave your cell phone there as well. No personal calls allowed during work time." The woman tapped her foot impatiently as Emma hung up her things. "Okay, let's have a look at you."

Marcie made a gesture with her hand indicating she wanted Emma to turn around. "A bit on the slim side; most of the customers like something to grab hold of. Oh well, we're short-handed so I guess you'll have to do."

Emma felt like she was a cut of beef that had been found wanting but kept her expression neutral. She could do this!

With a sniff, Marcie jerked her head towards the door. "Follow me and I'll show you the ropes."

Emma followed her through what seemed like a rabbit warren of corridors, passing offices, rooms marked 'Private', a large kitchen. Finally they stopped and Marcie drew open a heavy metal fire door and, for a moment, Emma thought she'd gone blind.

Slowly, her eyes adjusted to the poor illumination and she realized it wasn't actually dark. The light was slowly changing from blue to purple to red and back to blue only to cycle through the sequence again. She took a couple of running steps to catch up to Marcie who was talking to her.

"Do you have much experience?"

"I worked in a bar at college, not much since then."

"Well, like I said, we're short-staffed at the moment so you'd better be able to handle it. No one's available to bail you out. Three girls didn't turn up for work this week." Marcie moved behind the bar and pulled a round tray off a shelf. This she handed to Emma together with a small order pad and pencil. "To start you'll be serving drinks and food. You'll only get permission to offer other services once you've passed probation. That's two weeks from today."

"Other services?" She tried to keep her expression neutral but apparently wasn't completely successful.

Marcie gave her a hard look. "Waitressing doesn't pay that much. A lot of the girls need to supplement their income, right?"

Emma nodded while inwardly cringing.

"All activity must take place on the premises and the house gets eighty percent." Marcie leaned against the bar, arms folded. "It's optional but the boss likes the girls who earn him a little extra on the side."

Emma didn't quite know what to say to this revelation. Thankfully, Marcie kept on talking.

"You work three hours on fifteen minutes off. You can only use the restroom during those fifteen minutes." She took a page of white labels out of a cabinet, wrote 'Emily' on one and stuck it on a large brandy snifter. "This is for your tips. Again, the house keeps eighty percent."

Feeling sorry for women who had to work at jobs like this to keep body and soul together, Emma nodded again. "Do women often disappear? Er...I mean not show up without giving any notice?"

Marcie cracked the gum she was chewing. "Yeah, it happens from time to time, although not usually three together. It's mostly the young ones who don't come back." She looked Emma up and down, then nodded. "Okay, you're set to go. After your first break I'll show you around upstairs. You've got tables one through twelve." She pointed at a table plan next to the cash register. "Rob's on bar tonight – don't bother trying it on with him, though. I've hit on him ever since he started three weeks ago. Nothing. I think he's gay or something."

"Oh. Er...thanks for sharing that." Emma grabbed a tray, not really caring what the bartender's sexual orientation might be. She had a more important agenda than picking up men.

~~~

Over the centuries, Alex had been in many places of sexual entertainment and the Dusky Rose didn't even score a lowly one star on his mental scale of depravity. He wandered around the room occasionally watching the drag queen comic or the strippers but more often keeping close tabs on Emma.

He was discovering she had hidden talents. After he'd overcome his initial abhorrence of her outfit he began to appreciate how she looked in the minimal clothing. Not as voluptuous as some of the other girls, but there was still something about her that drew every man's eyes. She was like a lily in a garbage dump, unexpected, beautiful, exotic; one couldn't help but want to pick it up and test its scent.

Surprisingly, when the patrons reached for her, Emma managed to deftly avoid their groping fingers without ever appearing to do so. It was like a dance how she turned at the right moment to pick up a glass or take an order, leaving a questing hand hovering empty in midair. Alex slowly curved his lips and nodded in approval. Yes, his Emma was full of surprises. He knew she was no shy virgin but he had no idea she had the experience to handle this kind of situation.

After observing Emma for a while longer, he realized she was in no immediate danger and began to investigate the rest of the club. The lower level was unremarkable. A few private rooms with poker games being played; illegal from the looks of it but not unexpected. The kitchen was noisy, hot and smelled of fried foods. And the employee locker room was decidedly dismal from the broken tile on the floor to the cracked plaster and rickety overhead light fixtures. It was also in desperate need of a coat of paint; the pea green shade on the walls made him feel queasy. There was nothing of interest in the room, so he happily moved his reconnaissance upstairs.
~~~

At the top of the staircase he paused, noting the red carpeting, gilded mirrors and dark wooden wainscoting. If the decorator had been trying to capture the look of a brothel, they'd succeeded. Alex continued down the hallway. There were rooms along one side, the doors ajar enough to reveal they were bedrooms, as yet unoccupied. No doubt that wouldn't remain the case as the evening progressed. A stout door at the far end seemed promising and he moved closer, thankful that, as an angel, he was able to float above the carpeting; it looked decidedly dirty.

The door at the end of the hall sported a gold plaque labelled private and was secured with a deadbolt. Giving a smirk, Alex drifted through the wooden surface.

He found himself in an office occupied by two men. The one behind the desk wore a black silk shirt and dress pants, the other occupant looked like the hired muscle.

Muscle sat cleaning his nails with the point of a switchblade and Silk Shirt was reading the paper. Occasionally, one or the other would glance out a window that looked down on the bar below. Alex poked about the room, listened to the two men argue over sports and finally watched in disgust as Muscle went to check on the rooms used by the girls and their johns. The place was sordid but that was about it. Once again, he hadn't uncovered anything that would be helpful to Emma.

~~~

Emma kept a smile pasted on her face as she weaved her way between the tables, a heavy tray of empty glasses in her hand. Her feet hurt and she had a headache from the lights and loud music. Now she remembered why she'd quit her college waitressing job after just a few months.

As she set the heavy tray down on the bar, she checked her watch. Break time. Thank goodness.

Sinking down on a nearby stool, she kicked off one shoe to rub her foot.
~~~

"Killer heels." Another waitress paused beside her and gave the footwear an approving nod as she leaned against the bar waiting for her drink orders to be filled.

"In more ways than one," Emma moaned. She flicked a look at the other girl. Too much make-up but there was still a hint of youthfulness underneath it all. They were probably only a few years apart.

"Sore feet are the least of your worries around here."

"What do you mean?" Emma scanned the room and then gave the girl a quizzical look. "I can handle grabby old men."

The girl cast a quick upward glance towards a large mirror above the bar. It was obviously a mirrored window.

"The owner?" Emma tried to keep her voice from sounding too interested despite the fact she was dying to quiz the girl at length.

"Your orders are ready, Reena." The bartender—Rob—slid the laden tray towards the girl.

"Your name's Reena? I'm Emily." Emma reached out to shake hands only to realize the girl was already hefting her tray of drinks.

"Nice to meet you. Sorry but I've got to go. I'm not due for a break yet and if you take one early, you're docked double pay." Reena hurried away.

"The owners seem to have a lot of ways to make deductions from your pay. " Emma murmured, thinking it was little wonder that Montrose's accounts always showed a hefty profit.

"You don't like it, you work somewhere else." Rob wiped the counter, his face impassive.

"I'm not complaining. A job is a job in this economy, right?" Emma backpedalled not sure whose side Rob might be on.

Rob grunted and moved to serve a customer.

So much for getting any information from him, Emma sighed. It was still early though, and she could hardly expect these people to start pouring out their life stories to her. She'd have to earn their trust first.

Marcie passed by and raised a quizzical brow. Emma gave her a thumbs up and put her shoe back on. Time to get back in the trenches. A new group was sitting down at table eleven.

The rest of the evening continued in the same vein. She waited tables and whenever possible tried to strike up a conversation with the other servers. Beyond names, she didn't make much progress. When the night finally ended, she had to wonder if her idea of uncovering clues by working at the Dusky Rose was a good one or not. Still, it was only her first night and she had an entire week's leave of absence from work. Surely within that time she'd discover something useful.

As she left the Dusky Rose, snow began to fall, the soft flakes covering her coat in white as if Heaven were trying to erase the filth of the place from her. The fanciful thought brought a smile to her face until she thought she heard footsteps behind her. She quickened her pace, the end of the alley in sight. It was late but at least a street offered the hope of a good Samaritan who might offer assistance if she was actually being followed.

The sound of footsteps behind her continued and her heart began to pound. How far to the safety of a well-lit street? She lengthened her stride and tightened her grip on her purse, planning to use it as a weapon if need be. Her keys were already in her hand but just as she positioned them so they could be used to gouge an attacker, there was a scuffling sound behind her followed by a muffled cry.

She spun around and saw a man flat on the ground and Rob, the bartender, just a few feet away.

"Rob? Did you—?"

"Nope. I saw him behind you and then he doubled over like he'd been punched and dropped to the ground."

"Maybe he tripped?" Emma stepped closer to the recumbent body, trying to see his face in the gloom. He didn't look familiar.

"Could be. He's likely drunk." Rob prodded the man with his toe and was rewarded with a loud snore. "You know, you shouldn't leave by yourself. Wait for the others."

She nodded. "I wasn't thinking. I guess I was tired after my first night and just wanted to get home as fast as possible."

Rob scowled. "Not thinking can get you in trouble in this neighbourhood."

"I won't make the same mistake again." She gestured toward the snoring man. "Do you think he was following me or just walking in the same direction?"

"Who knows?" Rob shrugged then pinned her with a hard stare. "It's late. You'd better head home."

Emma rubbed her hands up and down her arms. "Yeah. Thanks for watching out for me."

"Like I said, it wasn't me."

~~~

Alex sat in a straight-backed chair and watched his superior circle around him. Michael's hands were clasped behind him, his expression tight.

"There was absolutely no need to attack that man, Alex."

"He was following Emma."

"He was simply a drunk on his way home. There was no malicious intent."

"But how was I to know that? This whole 'need to know' business—"

The look on Michael's face had Alex clamping his lips together and slumping in his seat.

Michael sighed deeply and sat on the edge of his desk. "I like you, Alexander, I really do. You're an excellent GA and your maverick streak has paid off in a number of cases but this time..." He shook his head. "You're not thinking. You're reacting."
~~~

Alex muttered a half-hearted apology. "Sorry."

Michael raised one brow. "No, you're not." He paused and then stood up, rounding his desk and pulling open a drawer. "I believe you need some retraining."

"Retraining?" Alex jumped to his feet.

"Yes. Some time to recall the benefits of using your mind first before your fists."

"What's that supposed to mean?"

Instead of explaining, Michael handed him a keycard. "This card will allow you access to the archives. We're moving all our files from parchment to digital. It's a slow process and the archivists are short-handed. They'll appreciate your assistance."

"Archives?" Alex felt his brows shoot upwards. "But I need to watch Emma when she's at the Dusky Rose!"

"Zeke's there."

"Zeke!" Alex felt his temper rising and struggled to keep it under control. Now was not the time to fly off the handle. Not when Michael was already accusing him of not thinking before he acted.

"That's right. Zeke will watch her."

"But I—"

Michael held up a hand. "After a hard day's work, most angels would head to bed but your evenings will be free to do as you wish."

"You know damned well I'll spend them watching over Emma!"

"Language, Alex," Michael chided. "You can watch but, remember, no contact. Your own eternity is at stake."

Alex stormed out of the room and the smallest hint of a smile curved Michael's mouth. Just a few weeks ago, Alex had emitted a tired aura, lack of sleep leaving faint shadows under his eyes. There was no evidence of that anymore. The Campbell assignment had certainly sparked something inside the man. A spark, however, always had the potential to cause an uncontrolled explosion.

Michael narrowed his eyes as he considered the possible outcome of this case. With a sigh, he rounded his desk and sat down. It wasn't only humans that had free will. Alex's choices would seal his fate. Hopefully he would chose well.

Chapter 9

Emma brushed a stray curl from her face, then rubbed her aching back. What had she gotten herself into? Carrying heavy trays of beer while wearing spike heels was playing havoc with her spine. And after four days on the job, she was no closer to figuring out what was going on with the Montrose account. She'd made some minor progress in that the other wait staff were slowly warming up to her but they'd not shared anything important to the case.

"What do you think of the new dancer?" Rob nudged her elbow out of the way so he could wipe the counter.

"Hmm?" Emma glanced towards the stage. "I don't know. I guess she dances okay."

Rob stared at the girl. "How old do you think she is?"

"I don't know." She turned and looked at Rob. "Why do you want to know?"

"No reason. She just looks sort of young."

"Marcie said she thought you were gay, not a weirdo."

Rob scowled at her. "It was just an idle comment." He shoved her tray at her. "Get to work."

Emma took the tray and watched as Rob moved down the bar to fill another set of orders. The man was always asking questions. It seemed odd. Maybe she should be investigating him. She tucked the idea into the back of her mind for further consideration and headed towards the far side of the room only to give a gasp and make a quick u-turn. Holy smokes! Her boss, Mr. Stapleton was here! If he saw her, she'd definitely lose her job at the accounting firm. Sure she'd taken a week's leave from work but she was positive the firm would frown on an employee working at a strip joint during off hours! Ducking behind a bedraggled Christmas tree, she pressed the tray to her chest. She didn't know what was worse; the idea of losing her job or the idea of Mr. Stapleton staring at her wearing this skimpy outfit. The very thought of Mr. Stapleton ogling her breasts made her feel queasy. What was she going to do?

Reena passed by and Emma grabbed her arm, pulling her into the shadows. "I need your help. Please!"

"What's the matter?" Reena gave her a suspicious look while pulling her arm free.

"See that guy at table eleven? Wispy, dark hair. Thin lips. Glasses."

Reena peeked between the branches of the tree. "What about him?"

"I can't let him see me. Can we trade sections?"

"Your ex?"

"Er…well…we have a history."

Reena looked at Mr. Stapleton again and made a face. "Eww. Good escape. I've seen him here before. He's creepy."

Mr. Stapleton frequented a place like this? She mentally shook her head. "So can we trade?"

"I guess. I'll have to tell Rob."

"Thank you *so* much." Emma breathed a sigh of relief.

"I had a shit-crazy ex once. I know what it's like." Reena gave her a genuine smile.

Emma didn't know whether to be grateful for the help or insulted that Reena thought she'd ever stoop to dating an old man like Mr. Stapleton! Well, at least it had helped her build a bond with the other girl. After giving one last glance at table eleven, Emma scurried to the other side of the room. The lighting was pretty dark and Mr. Stapleton wouldn't be expecting to see her here. Plus, she was dressed totally different from her usual prim office attire. Mentally crossing her fingers that she wouldn't be noticed, she returned to work, carefully keeping her back towards her boss.

<center>~~~</center>

Alex suppressed a tired yawn as he drifted through the door that led to the Dusky Rose's office. His eyes felt scratchy and the desire for just ten minutes of rest was almost overwhelming. Working day and night was harder than he'd imagined it to be. Thankfully, Michael seemed impressed with his efforts and had declared today his last day in the stuffy archives. Of course, the archangel had also given him a lecture on remembering to think first, to follow the rules and, of course, to keep his distance from Emma Campbell.

Yeah. Right.

Alex glanced out the window that overlooked the bar to check on Emma. She was still in sight. Good.

He returned his attention to the office and looked about wondering where he'd start searching tonight. He'd made a habit of checking it each evening, hoping to find some useful clue. Tonight things finally looked promising. Shirt had something beyond the sports page spread on his desk for once. Alex leaned over the man's shoulders and perused the papers. Emma had noticed something wrong with Montrose's accounting. Could there be a clue here? To his untrained eye there appeared to be nothing remarkable. Bills for liquor and electricity. A log of employee working hours and tips earned. He paused and stared at one of the pages again. Hmm... Was that why Emma had got herself taken on as a waitress? Did she think there was something shady about the wages? It would be a lot easier to figure things out if he could ask her directly rather than trying to second guess her motives.

Circling around the desk, he attempted to read the paper that Shirt was resting an elbow on. Damn, if only the man would move—

The phone rang and Shirt reached to answer it, removing his elbow from the papers in the process.

Alex grinned and started to read the paper only to have the phone conversation catch his attention.

"Stapleton?" Shirt leaned back in his chair. "I'm surprised to hear from you again so soon. I thought we'd agreed that contact should remain minimal."

Stapleton? Wasn't that Emma's boss' name? Alex glanced at the clock on the wall. It seemed awfully late to be making a business call.

Shirt was frowning. "A problem with an employee? I thought you'd dealt with the issue, scared her off … A new problem? … She's here in the club? Just a minute."

Shirt got to his feet and walked to the large window that overlooked the establishment below. Alex followed behind, scanning until he located Emma. She'd moved to a new group of tables since he'd last checked on her. Why the switch?

"Which girl? … Long, curly hair? Yeah, I see her." Shirt kicked the leg of the chair that Muscle was sitting in. The other man got to his feet, brows raised as he waited for an instruction.

Alex cursed. They were talking about Emma. Stapleton knew she was here, but how?

"I'll take care of it. Don't say anything to anyone about this." Shirt ended the call and then pointed towards Emma. "Pull that one's file and read it to me." He didn't look to see if Muscle was obeying his command. Instead, his eyes were locked on Emma.

Muscle found the requested papers. "Emily Cameron. Twenty-seven years old. On the application she wrote that she's worked as a server at fast-food joints and sports bars."

Shirt snorted. "Fake name and fake background. She works as an accountant. A nosey one who asks too many questions. That fool Stapleton was supposed to have handled the problem, obviously he's incompetent with anything beyond paper and a pencil.

"Want me to take care of her?" Muscle cracked his knuckles, a look of anticipation on his face.

"Yes. No. Let me think." Shirt tapped his lips thoughtfully. "Mr. M has been wanting some more goods. This might work out perfectly. We could rid ourselves of a pest and gain some brownie points at the same time."

"She fits the bill. He's into long hair right now."

Shirt nodded. "Bring her up here. We can lock her in one of the rooms overnight and— Damn."

"What's wrong?" Muscle stepped forward to look out the window and so did Alex.

"She's heading towards the employees' exit. Her shift must be over."

"I might be able to grab her off the street."

"No. Don't take a chance on being seen. Last time was too close for comfort. Follow her home in case the address on her application is bogus and then come back here." Shirt returned to his desk and sat down. "If she's looking for information she'll be back tomorrow. We'll get her then."

"And if she doesn't return?"

"We'll arrange something. Suicide. Falling through the ice on the river. But hopefully it won't come to that. She'd be the perfect Christmas present for Mr. Montrose." He leaned back in his chair, one corner of his mouth curling upwards. "What to get the man who has everything. A new bimbo to play with."

Muscle chuckled. "Yeah. He likes his toys. Too bad he breaks them so fast."

Alex stood frozen in place, Michael's words once again haunting him. *Emma is scheduled to die.* It couldn't be at the hands of a man like Montrose, could it? Bile rose in his throat as he imagined exactly how Montrose 'broke' his toys.

No. That couldn't be Emma's fate. It shouldn't be *anyone's* fate. He slowly clenched his hands into fists. First thing the following morning he was going to wring Michael's neck until he spilled all the information Heaven had on Peter Montrose and then he'd demand to know exactly when and where he had to be in order to save Emma!

~~~

Back at Emma's apartment, he sat on the edge of the vanity as she scrubbed herself clean. These past few nights it had been hard leaving her after her shift was over but now
~~~

that he didn't have to spend time in the archives anymore, he could indulge himself and spend some extra time in her company.

"Ugh. You know, Alex, just being in that place makes me feel filthy."

Of course, she didn't know he was there and he smiled to himself, pleased that she obviously hadn't forgotten him despite the mind-wipe that had occurred. It was purely selfish of him; he should want her to move on, to forget him and not grieve but it was nice to be remembered for a change. None of his other clients had ever remembered him once he was done with an assignment. They'd gone blissfully about their lives with no recollection of the man who'd saved them from peril. It had never bothered him before but now, now he desperately wanted to remain a part of Emma's life, even if it meant only occupying a tiny corner of her heart.

"I made a potentially useful contact though." Emma continued speaking. "Her name's Reena. She wasn't too keen on talking to me at first but I think I finally made a connection with her."

Alex could barely see Emma's outline through the translucent shower curtain. Hints of her curves, an occasional flash of bare arm as she reached for the bottle of shampoo. It was enough to stir memories of their one night together. Limbs tangled, kisses being exchanged.

He forced himself to look away and concentrate on her conversation.

"I nearly died when I saw Mr. Stapleton there. Who'd have thought a stuffy old man like him would go to a place like the Dusky Rose? It was lucky that I noticed him when I did. I'm sure he didn't see me." She paused and then gave a short laugh. "I guess everything really does happen for a reason; Stapleton being there gave me an 'in' with Reena."

Alex lifted an eyebrow at this piece of information. Now the telephone conversation he'd overheard at the club made more sense.

The shower curtain was pulled aside and Emma stepped out, tendrils of steam drifting around her. She reminded him of an angel walking through the mist, except angels were usually clothed. Emma most definitely wasn't. Water droplets were sliding down her naked body at a leisurely pace, caressing each curve and valley. Unable to tear his eyes away, Alex watched as she wrapped a towel around herself and then used another one to blot the water from her hair.

"Darn." Emma stopped drying her hair and frowned. "The shower head is still dripping. How many times have I asked the landlord to come and fix it?" Tossing the hair towel aside, she turned towards the tub, perhaps intending to check that the taps were really off, only to give a cry of surprise as her feet somehow slipped on the damp tiled floor and she lost her balance.

Alex sprang to his feet, grabbed her arm and pulled her upright a split second before her head would have made contact with the edge of the tub.

"Whoa!" Emma blinked, one hand pressed to her heart, the other gripping the edge of the vanity. "I felt really dizzy for a minute there."

"You need to be careful," Alex scolded as he soothingly rubbed her back. "Hitting your head on the tub could have been deadly."

Emma jerked away from his touch, her face paling as she looked around the room. "Alex?"

Oh shit! Alex stepped back, a cold feeling washing over him. He'd forgotten the no touching rule. A quick glance in the mirror revealed no reflection though. Perhaps Michael had overstated the gravity of the situation as a ploy to keep him in line?

Meanwhile, Emma brushed her damp hair from her face. "I guess working at the club was more stressful than I thought. For a minute I could have sworn I felt and heard you, Alex." She gave a self-deprecating laugh. "Pretty silly of me, wasn't it? After all, you're dead." The half-smile faded from her face as she spoke that last word. Picking up the discarded towel, she stared at it regretfully, her fingers slowly stroking the soft surface. "Alex, wherever you are, I hope you can hear me. I'm so sorry I dragged you into all of this." She sighed and leaned against the vanity. Bringing the towel up to her chest, she hugged it to her as if trying to seek comfort from the inanimate object. "If it wasn't for me, you wouldn't have been in that park, you wouldn't have been shot. You'd still be alive with your whole life ahead of you." She swallowed hard, her voice cracking. "I bet you wish you'd never met me."

Sadly, she finished drying and tugged on a nightshirt then padded to her bedroom. Alex followed, wishing he could tell her the truth. He'd never been truly alive. He had no idea what it must be like. Sure he walked among humans all the time, played the role like a pro but actually being alive, that would never happen. Being a guardian angel was all he knew. If it hadn't been for her, he'd never have known what it was like to eat pizza with someone you loved, to hold hands while walking in the snow, to share a kiss in a dark movie theatre.

Leaning against the doorframe, he watched her climb into bed and tug the blankets up around her neck. "I'll never regret having met you, Emma. You're special." He stepped closer to the bed, and smiled gently. "None of my other clients ever took notice of me. I was just some random person who happened to be there at the right time. When my job was done I was forgotten, but not you." He shook his head and stared across the room, lost in the memory of their time together. "You saw me, actually saw me, and took the time to get to know me. You made me feel…real. I'll treasure that for eternity."

He glanced down and noticed her shoulders were shaking. Damn. She was crying. Unable to resist, he eased down on the bed beside her. "Don't be sad. I'm still here. I'll always be here for you." He willed the thoughts into her mind and eventually her body relaxed and her sobs changed into the slow steady breathing of sleep. She rolled over to face him. In the dim light he could see her spiky lashes clinging to her tear-stained cheeks.

"I'm sorry." He brushed his hand over her head and then used his thumb to wipe a last remaining tear from her face. "I never wanted to make you cry."

Emma snuggled in closer to him and instinctively he wrapped an arm around her. A contented sigh escaped her and her lips curved upwards. "Alex..." She breathed his name in her sleep and his heart leapt in response.

Leaning back against the headboard, Alex absorbed the warmth of her body, inhaling the unique scent that was her. "Emma, whatever am I going to do with you?"

Chapter 10

Alex leaned over Michael's desk, glaring at the archangel. Michael gripped the arms of his chair, his face cold and stony.

"I don't respond to threats or foul language, Alexander. I suggest you retract that last statement. Now." The room trembled with that final word and Alex slowly straightened, a muscle twitching in his cheek.

"All right. I apologize for the wording…but not the sentiment behind it."

A moment ticked past and then another before Michael slowly nodded. "I'll let it go this time. But if you ever burst into my office uninvited again I won't be nearly as lenient. Take a seat."

Alex sat, his rage barely under control. "Those bastards are going to abduct Emma and give her to Peter Montrose!"

"That indeed might happen." Michael inclined his head.

"Might? Michael, I need to know exactly what's in the cards! If I don't, how am I going to protect her?"

"'What's in the cards.' An interesting turn of phrase." Michael leaned back in his chair, elbows on the armrests, fingers steepled in front of him. "Everyone is dealt a hand in life. Some seem to have a guaranteed win; Kings, Queens, Aces. Others have lowly threes and fours on their cards. They seem destined to lose but any skilled card player knows it's how you and the others at the table use the cards that matters. Any number of factors can affect the outcome."

"Quit the damned philosophizing." Alex slouched in his chair.

"It's true, though. Emma could have died tonight. Her foot slipped. She could have hit her head on the tub causing a brain bleed. Her life would have been over. *Should* have been over." He cast a meaningful look at Alex before continuing. "However, you were there, caught her in time and now she's safe. That lowly three card in her hand became a non-factor…for the second time."

"Second? Oh, you mean the bullet."

"Indeed. Twice now you've saved her life when the path of fate would have led her elsewhere."

"But how many other *lowly cards* does she have?"

Michael ignored his question. "And how many more *face cards* do you have, Alex? How many are you willing to use to spare her?"

"What?"

"You touched her, Alex." Michael leaned forward, resting his folded hands on the desk top. "You grabbed her arm. Rubbed her back. Wiped a tear from her face and then held her as she slept. Four contacts despite being told not to allow any to happen. You're endangering your own existence with this path of action you've chosen."

Alex frowned in momentary consternation, then brushed the incidents aside. "They were brief. No harm was done. I couldn't even see myself in the mirror."

"Really? She thought she heard you. Your voice is becoming more audible to her."

"Then I'll be careful not to speak around her." Alex replied tightly, not pleased with the turn the conversation had taken.

"And did you notice the room was steamy? It obscured the view. If she'd stared hard enough, known what to look for, she might have noticed you."

"But she doesn't know what to look for."

"And that was before you comforted her in bed. You'll be even more visible now."

"I'll stick to the shadows. Plus I'm wearing this hoodie." Silently, he mocked himself over this bit of self-delusion—as if a different style of clothing would prevent Emma from recognizing him. "Being seen is a non-issue. What I need to know—"

"What you *need* is to be more careful. Both in your actions and in your demands." Michael fixed a firm look at him. "I've been very tolerant of you bursting in here, breaking the rules, making ultimatums. If you'd been assigned Gabriel as a supervisor you'd find yourself pulled from the field so fast your halo would be left behind in the dust."

Alex compressed his lips, knowing there was some truth in the archangel's words. Gabriel had an even bigger stick up his ass than Michael.

"Just do your job, Alex. Use Zeke if you need to. He's chomping at the bit for something to do. And stop contacting Emma. This case does not require a hands-on approach. Your only purpose is to be with her on her final journey."

As he opened his mouth to speak, everything suddenly turned dark and then he found himself sitting on a park bench opposite Emma's apartment building. Alex cast an annoyed glance towards the sky. He hated it when Michael showed off his superior powers like that. Getting to his feet, he dusted the snow from his pants. At least Michael hadn't set him down in a tree or someone's backyard pond. That would have been damned cold.

And speaking of cold… Michael's parting words had set a chill in his heart. 'Your only purpose is to be with her on her final journey.' For all his efforts, Emma's fate remained the same. How could he stand by and let her die? How could he not intervene if he saw her in danger? How could he turn her losing hand into a win? He really didn't know the answer but he was going to keep trying as long as he was able.

The sun was setting, the streaks of orange and red that stained the sky were slowly being overtaken by the encroaching night. Lights began to appear in the windows of the apartments that lined the street and Christmas trees began to glow as people turned on seasonal decorations. He turned his attention to Emma's apartment. He'd put Zeke on guard duty again with a stern warning to tell him if she left the building or if anyone suspicious started hanging around. Since he'd heard nothing, he assumed it had been a quiet day. Unless Zeke had messed up again.

As if on cue, Zeke appeared next to him standing ramrod stiff.

"Hi, Alex!"

"Zeke." Alex bit back a sigh.

"Are you here for my report?"

"Report?"

"On Emma's activities."

"Oh. Sure."

With a flourish, Zeke materialized a clipboard and began to read from the pages on it. "At exactly seven-thirty, Emma woke up. She exited her bed from the left side, went to the bathroom and took a shower. The shower lasted fourteen minutes after which she—"

"Zeke?" Alex prayed for patience. "I don't need to know every single detail of her day. Just a general overview will do."

"An overview? Oh. Well, she spent most of the day on the computer."

"Anything else? Of importance that is."

Zeke furrowed his brow. "No. She was home all day."

"Good." Alex gave a nod, pleased that Emma had managed to stay out of harm's way.

"Good? You really mean that? You think I did good on an assignment?" A wide smile appeared on Zeke's face.

Alex stared at the young GA. He didn't have the heart to tell him otherwise. "Yeah. You did good."

"Gee, thanks, Alex. I can't wait to tell Michael what you said!" With that, Zeke disappeared.

Alex shook his head, thinking Zeke reminded him of an overgrown Labrador puppy. Well, Michael could pat the young angel on the head. He had more pressing matters to deal with.

Chapter 11

Saturday night in a sleazy bar. What fun.

Not.

Emma made a face as she stood at the kitchen serving window of the Dusky Rose, trying to block out the loud music that poured from the nearby speakers. Already she had the beginnings of a headache.

Shifting her weight to her other foot, she snuck a french fry from a customer's order and munched on it as she waited for the other plate to be prepared. The club's food was nothing to write home about but her stomach had been too in knots for her to eat earlier. She'd been off kilter all day.

It had started with her dream about Alex the previous night; it had seemed so real. This morning she'd been sure she could even smell his scent on the sheets, which was ridiculous of course. It was just the product of her overactive imagination.

Sadly, it wasn't her imagination that had produced the story on the newsfeed she'd read while sipping her morning cup of tea. Another missing woman and she'd been from this city. The facts shared by the police force had been sketchy, just the woman's name, Annabelle Henderson, her age, and the last date she'd been seen, which was, coincidentally, just two days before Emma had been hired at the Dusky Rose. It wasn't much but, given what she already knew, Emma was filled with a horrible sense of déjà-vu. Some digging through the Montrose papers she'd pilfered revealed a woman with a similar name on the Montrose payroll. Had the woman used an alias to keep her night job separate from her real life? Was Annabelle Henderson really Belle Hanson? Perhaps. And if so, that explained the opening at the Dusky Rose that Emma was now filling.

She'd spent the rest of the day thinking about the missing woman and plotting ways to gather more information about Montrose. Sadly, all the supposedly clever leading questions she'd planned on using had failed so far.

Marcie hadn't been forthcoming about the names of the other employees when Emma had asked earlier this evening. And Rob, the bartender, had hijacked her feeble attempts to question him with his own queries. She'd left him restocking his shelves and had gone in search of a different source of information. Emma ate another french fry while scanning the room, wondering who she could corner next.

Reena passed by and Emma gave her a friendly smile. That was a source she hadn't tried yet. The other girl's break was coming soon and thankfully it was still early enough in the evening that business was slow, although she knew the pace would pick up considerably as the night progressed. With any luck she'd be able to find some time for a conversation.

The cook dinged the bell indicating the order was ready. Emma grabbed the plate and added it to her tray then made her way across the room.

"Chicken wings, extra spicy, a burger with fries and two beers. Anything else?" Emma placed the dishes on the table and dodged the groping of one man only to feel another slide his hand along her thigh. She moved away, keeping the look of disgust from her face. "Sorry, sir. No sampling the merchandise."

"How much?" The man leaned back, rocking his chair on its hind legs as he looked her up and down.

"Sorry. Wrong time of the month." She stepped back.

The man appeared ready to protest when his chair suddenly collapsed and he tumbled to the floor, his plate of food landing on top of him.

Emma barely managed to keep from laughing. Thanking her lucky stars for his perfectly timed accident, she let the bouncer sort out the situation. If the guy was thrown out for breaking the furniture, it would serve him right. He had no business talking to her like that! The man was old enough to be her father, for heaven's sake!

"What happened over there?" Reena lifted a questioning brow as Emma leaned against the bar.

"That old guy was hitting on me." She shuddered and made a face.

Reena glanced toward the table and shrugged. "I've had worse."

"That must be…difficult."

Reena was quiet for a minute, staring at the glass of water she cradled between her hands, then nodded. "Yeah. But I need the money. My mother's sick and her medication is expensive. I send any extra I make to her."

Emma frowned. "Does she know the kind of work you do here?"

"Nah. She thinks I'm working as a nanny. And I was…at first."

"What happened?"

"The kid's father was hitting on me and his wife didn't like it. She raised her glass in a mock salute. "With no reference this was all I could find."

"I'm sorry."

"Hey, you do what you have to do, right?" Reena shrugged one shoulder. "It's not like there's a good fairy who's going to rescue you."

"You been here long?" Emma eased down onto the bar stool beside her.

"Almost a year."

"So you like it?"

"It's a job. I can't afford to be too fussy." Reena took a sip of her water. "What about you? This doesn't look like the type of work you're used to."

Emma used the same story she'd fabricated on her application. "I lost my job, too. The rent is due plus I want to be able to buy a ticket home for Christmas." She shrugged.

"I'd love to go home for Christmas." A wistful look came over the woman's face.

"Where's home?"

"South."

"Like Florida or Texas?"

"A bit farther than that."

"Ah." Emma noted the woman's accent, faint though it was. "Have you lived here long?"

"Long enough." A wary note entered the woman's voice.

"Sorry. I wasn't trying to be nosey. Just making small talk."

Reena nodded. "You're not so bad, you know. When I saw you on your first night I thought you looked really stuck-up."

Emma shook her head. "No. I was just scared spitless."

Reena laughed. "It's okay here as long as you stick to serving food and drinks. Rob's a bit full of himself even though he's only been here a while. And Marcie's tough but she's fine once you get to know her. Just make sure you avoid the boss. He reminds me of a rattlesnake."

"Thanks for the warning." Emma scanned the room. "Who else works here apart from those on shift tonight? Marcie mentioned three girls not showing up this week? It made me wonder."

"Suzy and Kim had the 'flu. It's going around."

"And the other girl?"

"Belle?" Reena looked away, the air of friendliness disappearing. "I guess she quit." Abruptly, Reena set her glass down and stood up. "I have to use the bathroom before my break's over. Talk to you later."

Emma studied Reena as she quickly walked towards the back. Why had she ended the conversation so suddenly? Did that mean she knew something? Had Belle really quit or had she disappeared?

"What were you talking to Reena about?" Rob appeared, a speculative look on his face.

"Nothing much. Just girl talk." Something about the bartender made her uneasy. She had gay friends so it wasn't his sexual orientation, if he was indeed gay like Marcie thought; but something about him had her radar pinging, though exactly what she couldn't say. Average build, gelled short brown hair, one small gold earring. He was good-looking, she supposed.

"That's all? She looked upset to me." Rob frowned.

We were both saying it would be nice to go home for Christmas." Emma shrugged. "You know how it is this time of year."

Rob raised one brow and Emma felt compelled to elaborate.

"Everyone wants the perfect Christmas the media keeps pushing. Snow, presents, a big meal, the whole family together, everyone getting along." Unexpectedly, she felt the prick of tears. She missed those family Christmases, but with her two sisters married and living on opposite sides of the country and her mom remarried it was hard to coordinate everyone. It had been three years since they'd spent the holiday together. And this year, with Alex gone, she'd feel more alone than ever.

Rob wiped at a spot on the counter. "The perfect Christmas? Is that what Reena wants?"

"Ask her yourself." Emma glanced at the clock and grabbed her tray. "I have to get to work." For a gay guy, he sure seemed interested in Reena. Yeah, there was definitely something 'off' about him.

Emma resumed her duties vowing to find another opportunity to talk to Reena when Rob wasn't around. She wouldn't put it past him to try and eavesdrop.

Chapter 12

Alex hovered in the shadows as near to Emma as he dared. He was being careful not to touch her or speak, Michael's warnings echoing in his mind. It was harder than he'd thought it would be. For one thing, she looked damned sexy dressed in those short shorts; the urge to span her tiny waist and pull her close for a kiss had almost been overwhelming. For another, seeing Emma working in a place like the Dusky Rose raised both possessive and protective instincts within him.

When that old geezer had propositioned her a few minutes earlier, he'd wanted to grab her by the arm and drag her from the place. Instead, he'd limited himself to knocking the chair out from under the man and dumping food on him. It had been satisfying to see the look on the guy's face, though punching him in his filthy mouth would have been even more rewarding.

I hope you noticed how I controlled myself, Alex mentally told Michael.

He resumed his patrol of the club. The guy he'd dubbed 'Muscle' was going to grab Emma tonight, but when and where? Definitely someplace secluded which ruled out the main part of the club. Upstairs? In the alley? He searched the main floor of the club but there was no sign of the thug. Did that mean the plan had been changed? Did he dare leave Emma unsupervised while he zipped upstairs to eavesdrop? Leaning against the wall, he considered his options.

"Hey, Alex, can I help?" Zeke suddenly appeared in front him and Alex jerked back in surprise, hitting his head against a wall sconce. The glass cover actually jiggled a bit, evidence that he was somewhat more substantial than he used to be. Thankfully the dim lighting and loud music appeared to have prevented anyone from noticing that the light fixture had moved on its own.

"What are you doing here?" Alex rubbed his head and hissed the question at the other guardian angel, mindful that Michael had said his voice would become more audible as he moved deeper into the state of being a shade.

"I was watching you. You seemed indecisive and—"

"Watching me?" Alex straightened and raised a brow, not pleased to have someone keeping tabs on him.

"Michael said you were one of the best and to stick close. That I could learn a lot from you." Zeke clasped his hands behind his back and stood staring straight ahead. "Awaiting your orders."

Alex bit back a sigh thinking all that was missing had been a 'sir'." Just what he needed right now; an eager young recruit. "Zeke, I don't..." He paused, a thought coming to mind. "I *do* have an assignment for you."

"Really? What is it?"

"Watch Emma while I go upstairs. Don't let her out of your sight, not even for a second. Let me know if anything happens."

"I'll let you know if anything happens." Zeke nodded as he repeated the instruction only to frown. "Anything such as...?"

"Anything beyond basic waitressing duties." Alex snapped, concern for Emma's safety leaving him little patience.

"Understood." Zeke saluted and then looked at him expectantly.

There's no damn way I'm saluting him, Alex grumbled to himself. He made a shooing motion with his hands. "Go. Get to work. I'll be back in a few minutes."

Zeke went on his way. Alex watched for a moment until he was satisfied that the man was following orders, which he was, to the letter. Good thing Zeke was invisible and completely permeable or Emma would have tripped over him. The fool was so close, he was almost breathing down her neck!

Shaking his head, Alex extended his wings and started to drift upstairs only to realize he was moving sluggishly, as if his ability to merely float between floors was on the fritz. And, he frowned; some of his feathers were coming out. He snatched them up as they drifted by and stared at them, a knot of concern forming in his stomach as the reality of becoming a shade settled in.

Irreversible.

Cease to exist.

His hand curled into a fist around the feathers before he slowly opened his hand and stuffed the bits of fluff into his pocket. This wasn't the time to be concerned about his own future. Emma was his priority. His own fate was irrelevant. He headed towards the stairs to ascend in a more human fashion.

Thankfully his ability to make his footsteps silent appeared to still be working. He made no sound as he climbed the stairs and walked down the hallway to the office. Passing through the closed door took a bit more effort than he was used to, rather like squeezing through an opening that was too narrow, but he made it. Breathing heavily, he wiped a drop of sweat from his brow; not something he'd want to do every day. It was worth it though, if it meant he could save Emma.

Muscle was there talking to Shirt. "I have everything ready. You say the word and I'll grab her."

"Let me confirm with Mr. M, first. We don't want to have to keep her here too long. Someone might notice something or hear the little bitch if she screams bloody murder."

Alex cursed as he listened to Shirt place the call. From what he could gather from this end of the conversation, Mr. M was ready to stop by and pick up his 'present'. The bastard would be there within the hour!

"It's a go." Shirt hung up and nodded at Muscle.

Muscle grinned. "I'll lure her into the back alley, drug her and tie her up. When Mr. M comes by we can toss her in the trunk."

"Don't rough her up too much. That's Mr. M's job. And make sure there are no witnesses." Shirt gave Muscle a pointed stare. "Not like last time."

Muscle tightened his mouth, apparently not pleased to have the incident mentioned. "I keep telling you, no one saw what happened with Belle. It was a stray cat that knocked over the garbage can."

"You keep saying that, but my gut is saying otherwise."

"The cops would have been all over us if they had even the slightest suspicion of what was going on. Have you seen any cops here?"

"No." Shirt conceded with a sigh. "I guess I'm getting jumpy. Six missing women in six months. The cops aren't stupid."

"Mr. M has the cops in his back pocket." Muscle leaned back against the wall and folded his arms.

"Some, but not all."

"Enough to keep the cops away from us. A few palms greased, a misplaced report…"

Shirt made a noncommittal sound as Muscle continued on with his theory.

"They're from all over the country. Plus they all worked at strip joints. What are the chances they'll ever connect the cases?"

"I didn't get where I am today by relying on chance."

"Come on, how much manpower do you think they're willing to put into investigating the disappearance of a few sluts?"

Shirt didn't reply. Instead, he walked to the window and stared down at the club below. "If the money wasn't so damned good I'd never have agreed to this."

Muscle grunted. "You oversee what? Half a dozen clubs? The money we make Montrose from this little sideline is double what the clubs bring in."

"That won't do us much good if we're all in jail."

"What gives with you?" Muscle pushed away from the wall, frowning. "You been listening to too many Christmas carols or something? We don't have time for you to have your own personal 'Scrooge sees the light' moment. Montrose will be here in less than an hour and you promised him a present."

Shirt turned back to look at his accomplice. "No change of heart, just cautious. Sometimes you need to lay low for a while. I'm feeling twitchy, like something is off." He rubbed his neck and looked around the room. "If I didn't know better, I'd say someone was here, breathing down my neck."

Alex drew back into the shadowy area near the filing cabinet. He was sure no one could see him but just in case, he'd err on the side of caution.

"I'm going to suggest that this one is our last sale for a few months. We quit using the Rose establishments as our source." Shirt returned to his desk. "Mr. Montrose has a wide variety of business interests. I'm sure there's another we can use to continue to supply our buyers with what they want."

Damn, Alex cursed under his breath. What had Emma stumbled upon? From the conversation he'd just overheard, it sounded like these two were somehow orchestrating the wholesale abduction of women, perhaps even selling them into white slavery. And Emma was next on the list!

Chapter 13

Looking up from the table she was wiping down, Emma noticed that Reena was standing in the corner and seemed on the verge of tears. Had a customer upset her? A quick glance around told Emma none of her tables needed her at the moment, and Rob was busy. Leaving the dishcloth on the table, Emma made her way towards the other girl.

"What's wrong, Reena? One of the customers giving you a hard time?" She studied the crowd again but no one was looking their way. "I can get the bouncer for you."

Reena shook her head. "No. It's the song."

Emma cocked her head and listened. The entertainment was between sets and a Christmas carol was playing in the background, oddly out of place in a sleazy club like the Dusky Rose. "Why does this song make you cry?"

"It was Belle's favourite. She said her mom always sang it to her when she was kid."

Belle! Did she dare press for more information? Emma tried to keep her interest from showing in her voice. "I don't understand. Belle liked the song." She gave a one shouldered shrug. "So what?"

"It's just…" Reena's face scrunched up and she shook her head.

Emma took half a step closer and placed a comforting hand on the other girl's shoulder. "Tell me what's wrong, Reena. Maybe I can help."

Reena hesitated, glanced around and then nodded. "Okay, but not here. Meet me in the back. Make sure no one sees you following me though. Especially Rob. He's too damned nosey."

"Okay."

The other girl darted away and Emma resumed cleaning the tables, slowly working her way toward the back room. The two other girls working the shift were on the floor so they could pick up the slack for a few minutes.

Rob was talking to the cook. Marcie was chatting up a customer. Emma slipped through the fire door unnoticed. The hall was frighteningly dark, the only illumination coming from bits of light that seeped out under the doors of two of the private poker rooms. Faint murmurs could be heard coming from them and she forced herself to tiptoe as she passed by.

Once she reached the locker room, she paused and took a deep breath to steady herself before gently pushing the door open. Reena was nervously pacing the room, her face pale and stained with tears.

~~~

Fate be damned! Alex knew he had to save Emma regardless of what Michael felt her destiny was supposed to be. Plus he had to ensure these guys were stopped before any more innocent women were abducted. A guardian angel couldn't allow others to be in peril. Sure a GA might have a specific assignment but duties extended to the general populace as well. At least that was what he was going to use in his defence if his actions were questioned!

Zeke suddenly appeared at his side interrupting his train of thought. "I've been watching Emma and I think she's veering from basic waitressing duties."

"What?" Alex blinked. "Veering from—"

"Basic waitressing duties. You told me to let you know if she did." Zeke smiled, looking pleased with himself.

"Exactly what is she doing? Details, Zeke. I need details."

"Ah! I understand." Zeke nodded. "Emma's heading towards the employees' room at the back. I think she's following that other girl, Reena."
~~~

Alex glanced out the window that overlooked the club. Sure enough, there was no sign of Emma. He willed himself downstairs but to his surprise he didn't move. Not even an inch. He was still in the office.

"What's the matter?" Zeke cocked his head to the side. "I thought you'd want to follow her."

"I do. I mean I want you to go first. I'll meet you downstairs in a minute." Alex ran his hand through his hair. This stupid shade business was messing with his abilities. He'd have to take the stairs like a regular person. Zeke, however didn't need to know about the predicament he found himself in.

"Sure. I'll be waiting for you." Zeke disappeared before Alex could speak.

Muttering under his breath, he looked around only to realize that Muscle and Shirt had gone. Damn!

~~~

"I'm here." Emma pushed the door of the employee locker room shut behind her and then looked expectantly at Reena. "What did you want to tell me?"

"It's about Belle. I know what happened to her." Reena's hands were shaking as she wiped tears from her cheeks.

Emma's heart began to beat faster and she had to force herself to remain calm. "I'm listening."

"It was last week. I went outside for a smoke. It wasn't my break time but the place was dead so I snuck out. No one saw me because I stayed back in the shadows, just in case. No point in advertising I was outside on my own in this neighbourhood, right?"

Emma silently agreed with her; it was decidedly a seedy part of town.

"Anyway, I heard this muffled noise, like someone calling for help and then scuffling feet. I peeked out and I saw two guys carrying Belle." Reena wrapped her arms
~~~

around her middle. "She was tied up and gagged. They threw her into the back of a van."

"What?" Emma gaped at her, completely forgetting the role she was supposed to be playing. "You saw that and yet you didn't call the police?"

Reena started to sob. "I know, but I was scared. I'm not exactly legal, you know? If I'm caught I can't send money to my mom for her medicine. She could die." Reena cried all the harder.

"Oh." Emma blinked. "I see, but…" She ran her hand through her hair. She couldn't keep silent about this, even if it meant Reena being exposed as an illegal immigrant. "An anonymous tip. You could do that."

Reena's eyes widened. "No. They can trace calls, everyone says so. If the police question me, I could end up being deported!"

"All right. I understand. Umm… We'll call Crime Stoppers." She moved towards her locker, intent on getting her cell phone from her purse. "Did you hear the men say anything? Could you identify them?"

"It was Jim Perry, the boss, and Frank."

"Frank? Is he the big muscle-bound guy?" Emma recalled the man she'd met when she first arrived at the club. No one had introduced her to anyone; in a place like this, the formalities weren't that important apparently.

"Yeah, Frank Darrell. He's in charge of upstairs, makes sure things don't get too rough and that the house gets its percentage."

Emma grimaced with distaste but pressed for more information. "Can you tell me anything else?"

"Well, the guy in the van gave Jim a package. It was full of money. I saw him counting it." Reena frowned, eyes narrowed as she searched her memory. "Oh, and they said something about some country. I don't remember the name but I do remember thinking it was somewhere in the Middle East or maybe one of those countries that Russia used to rule."

"You know what this is, don't you, Reena?" Emma stared at the other girl, her eyes wide as all the pieces fell into place. "I bet it's some sort of white slavery or a sex slave racket and we've landed right in the middle of it."

"I saw a movie about that just a few weeks ago," Reena gasped.

"I saw it, too. And we don't want to end up like those poor characters!" Emma looked around trying to decide what to do. "Okay, here's the plan. If we stay here much longer someone is going to notice we're missing. You head back and start waiting tables. If Rob asks where I am, say I'm feeling queasy."

"That should work," Reena nodded, wiping the tears from her face. "Stomach 'flu has been hitting everyone here."

"I'll place a call to the police and—"

The door swung open before she could finish speaking. It was Frank. "What are you doing in here, Reena? It's not your break. Get back on the floor and start earning us some money."

Reena appeared about to say something but Frank pinned her with a look. "Be a shame if the police learned there were illegal immigrants working here, wouldn't it?"

Reena paled, her eyes wide. After shooting Emma a worried look, she slipped past Frank and disappeared down the hallway.

Emma pasted a smile on her face. "I'd better head back, too."

"No. We need to talk." Frank shot out an arm, blocking the exit.

"W…what about?" Emma was sure she could hear her knees knocking together.

Frank pushed the door shut. "You're new here but you know the rules. Breaks are every three hours. You've only been working two."

"Sorry. I forgot. I won't do it again."

"Girls who forget need to be taught a lesson."

"A lesson?" Her voice came out as a squeak.

Frank stepped closer and smiled, if the twist of his lips could be called that. She swallowed hard and lifted her chin even as she backed away.

"Reena knows you're back here with me."

"She won't say anything. And if she does ask about you, I'll tell her I fired you." He pulled a rag and a small bottle from his pocket.

"What's that? What are you going to do to me?" Dumb, dumb question, she muttered to herself. You know what he's going to do!

"Just a little something to keep you quiet. We don't want to bother the customers."

Emma stepped back again and bumped into the locker. The metal clanged as she made contact with it, the coldness of the surface quickly penetrating her almost non-existent top. A glance towards the exit told her there was no way she could cover the distance. It was, however, her only option. She darted towards the door.

Two steps into her escape attempt and Frank grabbed her arm, yanking her towards him.

"No! Let me go!" Her back hit his chest and she struggled to escape, using her killer heels to stomp on his foot. Unfortunately, the term 'killer' was a misnomer. He merely grunted and wrapped his arm around her waist, drawing her closer so that his belt buckle dug into the small of her back.

Crap! She was in big trouble now and, barring a miracle, there was no chance of rescue!

Chapter 14

Alex arrived downstairs to find Zeke hiding behind the saddest excuse for a Christmas tree that he had ever seen. Why was the man playing hide and seek at a time like this? It wasn't like anyone could see him!

"What are you doing and where is Emma?"

"Shh!" Zeke glared at him and then pointed towards the nearby bar.

Peering through the dusty branches Alex saw Reena being questioned by the bartender, Rob.

"Where's the new girl?" Rob had his arms braced on the bar.

Biting her lip, Reena glanced nervously towards the backroom and then looked away.

Rob compressed his mouth. "Taking an early break? What is it with you girls? I should—"

Reena twisted her fingers, tears welling in her eyes. "She's in the backroom with Frank. I think…I think she might be in trouble."

Rob frowned, shot a glance towards the back and then rolled his eyes. "Get to work. You're all a bunch of whiners." He shoved a tray at the girl. "Go take care of table six."

"Bastard," Zeke whispered.

Alex agreed but didn't stick around to hear the rest of the conversation. All he cared about was that Emma was in trouble. Leaving Zeke behind, he hurried down the hall towards the employees' locker room.

The door of one of the poker rooms swung open, cigar smoke swirling around the person who exited. It was Marcie carrying a tray of empty glasses. Alex barely remembered in time that he was no longer completely permeable and twisted to dodge around her. As it was the tray she was carrying brushed against him, wobbled in her hand and then flipped onto the floor, glasses crashing into pieces. Damn. Being a shade was trickier than he'd thought it would be. As a GA he'd never had to remember to walk around anything.

"Sorry." He muttered the apology as Marcie gave a squeak of surprise. There was no time to stop and help though. Who knew what trouble Emma might be in?

When he arrived at the locker room, he could hear voices inside and rushed to enter only to bounce off the door. What the—? He tried again, with slower, more deliberate movements but he still couldn't pass through the panel.

"Dammit, Michael, this is not the time for this shade stuff to kick in." He tossed the complaint upwards and then, not caring if anyone thought it odd or not that a door was opened by an invisible hand, he gave the knob a decisive twist and stepped inside.

For a moment he froze at the sight that met his eyes. Muscle had Emma pinned against him and was unsuccessfully trying to press a cloth to her mouth as she thrashed her head about.

"Let me go!" Emma squirmed this way and that, then dropped her weight causing Muscle to stagger for a moment.

Alex sprang into action, pulling Emma free before taking a swing at Muscle's gut.

"Oomph!" Muscle doubled over and Alex shoved him backwards over the bench and into the lockers. A resounding clang accompanied a groan as the big man slid to the ground.

Alex spun around to see how Emma was doing. She was pressed against the locker, staring at him with wide eyes in the middle of an unnaturally pale face. "Alex?"

He took one step toward her then stopped as understanding hit him. "You can see me?"

"Alex, you're a...a...ghost!" A mixture of shock and fear swept over her face and she slid along the lockers, increasing the space between them.

His heart twinged as he realized she was afraid of him and he gentled his voice. "No. Not a ghost." He glanced around, noticed a streaky, cracked mirror on the far wall and saw a translucent image of himself staring back. "I'm a shade."

"A shade?" She blinked then shook her head. "Shade, ghost, whatever. I can see you. Hear you. But you're...dead."

"No. Not really." He gave a crooked grin and took a tentative step closer, all the while gauging her reaction. "I was never really 'alive' in the human sense so I couldn't die."

"Never alive? But I saw you. Touched you. Made love with you." She swallowed hard. "And I saw you...die. I mean there was a gunshot and you fell down and there was blood everywhere and...and..." She ran a shaky hand through her hair. "Oh gosh, maybe I really am crazy, like the police said."

"You're not crazy. I'm really here. And there's no need to be afraid. I'm the same person I was before, just a bit more...transparent." Alex slowly stretched out his hand towards her. She watched him, a hint of wariness still in her eyes but she didn't recoil. He smiled and took her hand in his, then pressed a kiss to it.

Emma stared in obvious wonder at their joined hands. "I can see my own hand through yours." He squeezed lightly and she wiggled her fingers. Shifting her gaze to his face, awe filled her voice. "I felt that. I can feel *you*!" With her free hand, she reached out and touched his cheek. For a moment her hand rested on his flesh before passing through him as if he were nothing but air. "What?" She gave a gasp and jerked backwards. "But, a second ago—"

Alex shook his head ruefully. "I'm a shade, a state between being an angel and a corporeal being. I can touch you, but, for now, you can only touch me for a short period of time before I begin to evanesce."

"Angel? What? I don't understand."

"It's complicated. Suffice to say I started out as your guardian angel, then I became a shade – the state I'm in right now, but the more contact we have, the more 'real' and solid I'll become."

"I won't pretend that makes any sense to me but if contact is what it takes to make you real then I'll do my part." She threw herself against him, her arms wrapping around him as she held him tight. "Oh Alex, I've missed you!"

For a moment he held himself stiff, resisting the urge to gather her closer.

'No contact' Michael had said.

But Michael didn't have a warm woman hugging him. A woman he loved. Oh hell, in for a dime, in for a dollar. With a sigh, he gave in, returning the hug, pressing his cheek to the top of her head. His skin began to tingle just like when he'd shaken Michael's hand and he watched as his arms became more and more solid in appearance. Just as the archangel had predicted, extended contact with Emma was changing him into a corporeal being. Well, if he was going to end his existence, this was the way to go.

A large, beefy hand grabbing his shoulder interrupted his thoughts and spun him around. Damn. Muscle had revived.

"I don't know who the hell you are, buddy, but where you're going, it won't matter." With that the man swung at Alex's chin, his fist hitting its target with full force.

"Oof!" The blow caused Alex's head to snap back and he gave a cry of pain as he staggered to the side. Who'd have thought being corporeal would hurt so much! Before he could gain his balance, Muscle hit him again, sending him careening into the lockers that lined the other side of the room. Darkness crept into the edges of his vision, the room seeming to swim before him as his legs began to buckle beneath his weight.

Over the metallic clatter, he could hear Emma scream and his blurry vision gave him a glimpse of her flinging herself at the man. "Stop it! Leave him alone!"

Muscle shoved her aside as if she were a pesky fly. "First him. Then you."

As Emma stumbled and fell over a bench, Alex gave a roar of rage. No one could hit his woman and not suffer the consequences! Still shaken from Muscle's punches, he nevertheless launched himself at Muscle, intent on ramming his shoulder into the man's stomach. Just as he started his head-long run at Muscle, the door burst open and the bartender came rushing in. Shit! Two against one and, it would seem he'd lost all his powers.

"Zeke!" Alex roared the other angel's name even as he hit the wall of solid flesh that comprised Muscle's body. "I need some help here."

The force of Alex's blow was enough to cause Muscle to lose his balance and both men went crashing to the floor. Somehow Alex ended up underneath.

"I'm here, Alex." Zeke appeared kneeling beside him. "What can I do?"

"Get this lug off me!" Alex wheezed as he pushed against the recumbent man. The fellow had to weigh at least three hundred pounds!

Zeke grabbed Muscle around the neck and yanked.

"Gah!" Muscle gave a strangled cry as his head was jerked backwards. "Who's there?" He reached backward as if to grab his assailant but his hand passed through Zeke. Giving a frustrated growl, he shook his whole body rather like a large dog and managed to fling Zeke to the side.

As the man clambered to his feet, Alex took the opportunity to scuttle backwards gasping to regain the breath that had been knocked out of him. Damn, if he'd still been an angel, oxygen wouldn't have been so important!

Zeke tapped Muscle on the shoulder then laughed as the man spun around, fists raised only to freeze with a puzzled expression on his face when he failed to see anyone there.

Alex's snort of amusement quickly changed to one of anger when he looked beyond the duo to where Emma was.

Rob was approaching Emma, one hand outstretched. Recalling how the bartender had responded to Reena's appeal for help a moment earlier, his vision turned red. The bastard! Taking a running leap, Alex jumped on Rob's back taking them both into the mirror on the wall and the small sink mounted beneath it. The sink broke loose under their weight and water began to spray in every direction.

The water made the floor slippery and Rob's feet skidded, causing both of them to fall to floor. Alex managed to roll over and gain his footing first. He shook his now wet hair from his eyes and grabbed Rob by the collar, dragging him to his feet. The bartender wasn't giving up so easily, however, and aimed a kick at Alex's knee.

Nimbly avoiding the blow, Alex slammed the man back against the wall. Teeth bared, he drew back his arm, intent on delivering a knock-out blow to the bastard's chin.

"Alex, no!"

Zeke shouted the warning from across the room and Alex hesitated for a split second, flicking a glance in the other angel's direction. It was enough to allow Rob to break free. With a frustrated growl, Alex began grappling with the man once again.

~~~

Emma sputtered as water hit her in the face, soaking her clothes, her hair, the floor. Had the whole world gone mad? One minute she was hugging Alex, who she thought was dead or at least a ghost and then he suddenly seemed to become 'solid' in her arms. Just as she was about to comment on the change, Frank reappeared and started a fight only to unexpectedly forget about Alex and begin taking swings at thin air. And now Alex and Rob were fighting. While she didn't really like Rob, she hadn't pegged him as one of the bad guys. Alex seemed to feel differently though and if Alex was against him, then so was she!
~~~

Yanking off her shoes, she gripped one in each hand, holding them raised so the spike heels could be used as weapons.

"Alex, stay still." She demanded as she danced around the two men, looking for an opening where she could get a good whack at Rob.

Suddenly, Alex's arm jerked backwards as if pulled by some invisible hand.

"Let me go!" Alex growled as he struggled to free his arm from some unseen source.

Rob took advantage of Alex's preoccupation and aimed a kick at his stomach.

As Alex doubled over, Emma gave a cry of rage and launched one of her heels at the bartender only to have the shoe mysteriously hover in the air and then drop harmlessly to the ground.

"Zeke, what are you doing?" Alex shouted.

"Zeke? Who's Zeke?" Emma looked around. The only other person was Frank who was watching the proceedings with wide eyes and hands raised to form a cross as if hoping to ward off evil.

"What?" Alex continued to talk to thin air. "You heard him talking on his cellphone and he's an undercover cop?" He turned to look at Rob in surprise.

"A cop?" Emma swung her gaze towards Rob.

"A cop?" Muscle seemed to snap out of his trance.

"Indeed." A voice from the exit to the back alley had everyone turning sharply. It was the club manager and another man who Emma recognized as being Mr. Montrose from pictures she'd seen in the files at work. Both had guns pointed in their direction.

"James," Mr. Montrose spoke, "it would seem you've been harbouring a viper."

"Frank, explain what's going on here." The man, who seemed to be the Dusky Rose's manager, cocked an eyebrow in his side-kick's direction.

Frank stumbled through an explanation of sorts. "I was going to grab the girl but that guy," he pointed at Alex, "suddenly appeared out of nowhere. And then…" Frank paused and wet his lips. "Weird shit started happening."

"Weird shit?" James didn't look impressed.

"Yeah. Someone…something…grabbed me but when I turned around, no one was there. And then her shoe, it just stopped in mid-air and…" His voice trailed off and shuffled his feet.

Mr. Montrose narrowed his eyes. "James, it would appear your *assistant* has been drinking, is delusional, or both."

"I agree." James frowned. "Frank, quit babbling. You sound like you're concussed or something. Grab the merchandise and throw her in Mr. Montrose's trunk. I'll take care of these two." He used his gun to gesture that Emma should move. "Step away from your boyfriend unless you want me to blow his brains out right in front of you."

"Emma, don't!" Alex warned.

She flicked her eyes between Alex and Montrose, her stomach clenching.

"You or him, baby." James levelled his gun.

Emma compressed her lips, her eyes pricking with tears. Herself or Alex; there really was no choice. She tried to speak, her throat so tight the words wouldn't come out. She swallowed and tried again, her voice cracking as she finally delivered her message. "I love you, Alex. I can't let you die again." Going with Frank and Montrose would buy Alex a few minutes and maybe in that short period of time a miracle would happen. She gave him one last look, knowing she'd never see him again, hoping her love for him was showing in her eyes. Tremors shook her body as, with leaden feet, she walked towards Frank, trying not to think about what Montrose had planned for her.

Rob narrowed his eyes. "This place will be surrounded by cops any minute."

"Then I guess I'd better kill you quickly." James said.

"Zeke!" Alex hissed the word just as the locker room door opened and Reena stepped in.

"Emma, Marcie's wondering where you…" The waitress's voice trailed off as she took in the scene before her. "Oh my—" She started to step backwards.

"Get rid of her before she tells anyone what she's seen," Montrose demanded. James swung his gun towards Reena.

"No!" Emma cried lunging towards the gunman.

"Emma, stay back!" Alex shouted rushing forward.

"Duck!" Rob yelled as he dove towards Reena.

James's gun unexpectedly jerked upwards, the bullet hit the ceiling near the overhead light fixture causing it to come crashing down in a shower of plaster chunks and debris.

Emma screamed as she felt herself being grabbed around the waist and dragged towards the door. Through the clouds of dust, she could see Alex on the floor, bits of broken glass surrounding him and blood dripping from his forehead. Her heart lurched in her chest.

"Alex!"

Chapter 15

Alex pushed himself to his knees, coughing at the dust that swirled around him. His head throbbed and there was a ringing sound in his ears, almost like a siren. Or was it a siren? Hell, who cared? Those goons had just nabbed Emma and he had to save her. "Zeke, follow her!"

"I'm on it." Zeke zipped out the door while Alex struggled to his feet.

James was on the ground, unconscious from all appearances. To the side, Rob was helping the waitress up, a look of concern on his face.

"Reena, are you okay?" Rob brushed at the plaster dust that coated her. She nodded, shaking but appearing fine otherwise.

"Do you have a car here?" Alex grabbed the cop's arm.

"Yeah. Wh—"

"Come on." Alex dragged the man towards the door. "We have to follow them."

Rob took a last glance at the waitress. "Reena, tell Marcie what happened. The cops should be here any minute to deal with this scum." He punctuated the sentence by nudging James with his foot. "Here," he picked up James' gun and handed it Reena. "If he comes to just point this at him."

Reena gingerly took possession of the firearm and was just starting to nod in agreement when Alex dragged the other man through the back door into the alley. A set of taillights could be seen about a hundred feet away, turning left onto the street.

"There they are!" Alex cursed his lack of angelic abilities. Just a few days ago he would have simply appeared in Montrose's vehicle. Now he was forced to rely on a human for help. Dammit, he didn't even know how to drive! "Where's your car?" He dragged his hand through his hair in frustration while shouting at the cop beside him.

"Over there." Rob pointed to an old beige sedan and they both took off running to the nearby vehicle. The doors were barely closed when Rob hit the gas and took off in pursuit. Alex braced himself with one hand on the dashboard, scanning the street ahead for signs of Montrose's car.

Traffic slowed their passage and Alex cursed. "I thought you were a cop. Why don't you turn on your siren?"

"Undercover. No siren, no radio. Can't have anything in the car that would give me away."

Alex nodded in acknowledgement, then gave a shout and pointed. "There! Isn't that them?"

"I see them." Rob smoothly switched lanes. "Looks like they're headed towards the airport."

"I bet Montrose has a private plane." Alex's jaw was clenched so tightly he had trouble speaking. "If they manage to take off, we might never find Emma."

"Don't worry. He's not getting away." Rob pulled a cell phone from his pocket and tossed it to Alex. "Call the police. Ask for the captain and use the code word 'kid-stuff'; that will get you put through"

"Code word?"

"I'm undercover." Rob flicked a glance his way. "And not everyone on the force can be trusted. Some are on the take to guys like Montrose."

Alex nodded and placed the call, relaying the information Rob told him.

"Your captain said he's sending some cars to intercept." Alex took a deep breath and prayed it would be enough, that they'd be able to set up a road block or something that would stop the car ahead of them. Just in case...

"Zeke," he muttered quietly hoping that Rob would think he was praying under his breath. "Do something to stop that car." He kept his gaze fixed expectantly on Montrose's vehicle but there was no sign of it slowing down. In fact, the distance seemed to be increasing. Why wasn't Zeke carrying out his job? Or maybe the GA couldn't hear him. A sick feeling grew in Alex's stomach as he realized that he might not be able to communicate with other angels anymore. Was he completely alone now with no one to help him?

Just as he was beginning to despair, the car in front of them began to fishtail wildly.

"Looks like they've hit a patch of ice." Rob decreased his speed, his hands tightening on the wheel. "Brace yourself."

Alex watched in horror as Montrose's car began to spin completely out of control. He was barely aware of Rob struggling to keep their vehicle from doing the same. All he could think of was that Emma was in the car ahead and it was careening straight towards a concrete barrier!

One minute the other car was hurtling forward and the next it was a crumpled mass of metal.

"Emma!" Alex threw his door open, uncaring that Rob hadn't completely stopped the car. He stumbled from the vehicle and raced towards the crash site, slipping and sliding on the icy roadway.

Smoke filled the air; the wail of sirens grew louder by the second. Other cars stopped and a small crowd began to gather. Alex saw none of this. His eyes were fixed on Emma. She'd been thrown from the vehicle and was lying in the snow, a trickle of blood dripping from her mouth.

No.

She couldn't be.

He stepped closer taking in the unnatural angle of her limbs, the stillness of her body.

A sick feeling of dread filled him as he recalled the day he'd been shot and lay bleeding in the snow as Emma cried over him. Only now their positions were reversed and Emma had no angelic abilities to survive a fatal injury.

His legs grew weak and he fell to his knees at her side. "Emma? Emma!"

There was no response.

She's scheduled to die... The dreaded words reverberated through his mind.

His vision blurred, an unaccustomed wetness trickling down his face. He struggled to breathe as a gut wrenching pain filled him, squeezing his heart.

He stretched out a trembling hand to touch her but someone caught his arm.

"I'm sorry, Alex." It was Zeke. He was shaking his head, a sorrowful look on his face.

Alex turned on him, his voice hoarse with rage. "Why? Why didn't you stop the car like I told you to? Are you so caught up in following Michael's damned orders that you couldn't have done something?" He surged to his feet, grabbed the GA's shoulders and shook him with all his strength.

"Stop the car? You told me to follow her. You never said—" Zeke stared at him wide-eyed making no effort to defend himself against Alex's physical assault.

"Alexander, release him at once!" Michael suddenly appeared on his other side and shoved him back.

"Michael?" Shock stilled Alex for a moment. Michael never left Heaven.

"Yes. I'm here. Your behaviour dragged me from my office in the middle of a very important meeting." Michael scowled.

"It's his fault." Alex glared at Zeke. "I told him to stop the car—"

"He didn't hear you, Alex." Michael shook his head sadly. "You're a shade. Your angelic abilities are gone."

"But I can see you. And Zeke can hear me now." Alex stared at the two angels who flanked him and then glanced around. Rob was standing beside him using his cell to call for an ambulance but seemed completely oblivious of the two angels. Actually, he seemed oblivious of Alex as well. "What's going on?"

Michael sighed. "I've temporarily blocked the three of us from view and applied a limited mind-wipe. When we're done here you'll become visible again but no one will notice you suddenly reappearing." He held up a silencing hand when Alex would have spoken. "Zeke, you can go home. We'll debrief tomorrow."

Zeke turned to go, then seemed to think better of it. He placed his hand on Alex's shoulder. "I'm really sorry about Emma. She seemed like a good person."

Alex nodded, as he watched the young GA dematerialize. "Yes, she was a good person." The anger had dissipated from him. Now he felt cold, numb, his brain hardly able to process the words he was trying to speak. Emma was dead. Unfamiliar tears stung his eyes. "I tried so hard to save her, Michael."

"I know you did."

"I just wanted her to be happy. To be safe. I didn't care what happened to me." He stared down at Emma's broken body. He'd never lost a client before. Never lost someone he *loved* before.

"You risked everything for her." Michael paused, his brow furrowed. "And she did the same for you when she went with Frank. You're two of a kind, both willing to sacrifice the best cards in your hand for each other."

He looked at Michael, barely registering what the man had said. Guilt was eating away at him. "You shouldn't have put me on this case. Another GA might have saved her."

"No, Alex. It had to be you. I could see you were getting restless, that you needed a change."

"And so you sent me here? To meet my soulmate only to lose her?" He dragged his hand through his hair in disbelief. He was shouting now but he didn't care. "Did you know this would happen?"

Michael inclined his head. "You knew the assignment was to help her on her way to the next plain. However, nothing is certain in this life. Everyone has free will, even guardian angels, and there are always several paths someone might take. But yes, I had a strong inkling that this was in the cards. "

"Then why?"

"Would you have preferred to never have known her?"

Alex thought for a moment then shook his head. "No."

"It would have been wrong of me to shelter you. Emma was what you needed and you were what she needed. And both of you were needed to stop Montrose." Michael gestured to the side and Alex observed Montrose being cuffed while Frank was zipped into a body bag. "Do you remember a conversation you had with Emma when you first met? She said she wanted to leave the world a better place for her having been in it."

Alex blinked and opened his mouth to question how Michael knew about that conversation but Michael continued talking.

"You can take comfort in knowing that she achieved her goal. Between the two of you, you've saved a lot of women from a dreadful fate."

"What about Shirt? I mean James?"

"He's been arrested. The backup Rob called in at the club have arrived and dealt with him. And before you ask, the girl, Reena, will be fine."

Rob walked by, completely oblivious to the angels in his midst and Alex gestured towards him. "What was his role in all of this? Was he investigating Montrose as well? Would the bastard still have been caught if Emma hadn't begun poking around the Dusky Rose?"

"No. Rob's presence was a mere coincidence. He *was* working undercover but his case was underage workers."

"Oh."

Michael's eyes grew distant for a moment and then he nodded. "Reena and Rob quite likely have a future together, if they make the right choices."

Alex didn't reply. Choices. Had he made the wrong ones or the right ones? Would he ever know? Not likely. At least Emma would be happy in Heaven. She'd been too good a person not to get a ticket straight through the proverbial pearly gates. Unfortunately, he'd not be there to greet her. He was a shade now. In a few hours he'd cease to exist.

"Take care of Emma when she gets to Heaven, Michael." He turned his attention back to where Emma lay. "Show her around. Make sure she learns to fly." He smiled sadly, thinking of how cute she'd look with a halo resting among all those curls.

"Don't worry, she'll be well taken care of," Michael promised.

"Thanks."

Slowly, Alex sank to his knees. Stretching out his hand, he brushed the hair from her forehead and trailed the back of his hand down her cheek. "I love you, Emma. I love you so much. Never forget that." Bending forward he pressed a final kiss to her lips.

"Over here!" Rob yelled beside him and Alex gave a start.

He looked around. Michael was gone. Two ambulance attendants were rushing towards Emma.

"Hey buddy, I know she's your girlfriend but you need to step aside." Rob was pulling him away. "They'll patch her up. Hey guys, can he go in the ambulance with you?"

Alex blinked. Patch her up? She wasn't dead? What was going on?

Chapter 16

Alex kept his arm protectively around Emma's shoulders as they rode the elevator up to her apartment for the second time since all hell had let loose. Due, he supposed, to some heavenly intervention, it turned out Emma merely had a concussion plus some scrapes and bruises despite having been thrown from the car during the crash. Everyone said it was a miracle she hadn't been killed. Beyond a silent prayer of thanks, Alex hadn't made any comment about Emma's survival since he was pretty sure he knew what had really happened. Instead, he'd stuck to her side as she was treated at the hospital and had then escorted her home with instructions to keep a close watch on her.

"That won't be a problem," he'd whispered to her during the ride home in the taxi.

Emma had merely smiled and snuggled closer.

Of course, they'd barely settled in to her apartment when they'd been called into the local precinct to answer questions and make their statements. Despite Alex's protests that Emma needed rest, the detectives had kept them for the rest of the day.

Now Emma leaned against Alex as they rode the elevator up to her apartment. "I can't believe we spent almost the whole afternoon sitting in the police station."

"The wheels of justice turn slowly," Alex murmured as he stifled a yawn.

"They weren't turning at all from what I could see."

"Well, it took some time for Zeke to set up the selective mind-wipes. He's not very good at them yet and it took him a few tries." Alex gave a half smile as he thought of the young GA. Zeke might make a decent guardian angel one of these days. He tried hard and had a good heart. Hopefully, Michael would find someone to show him the ropes.

"Zeke, he's the invisible guy who stopped me from hitting Rob in the head with my shoe, right?"

"Right."

"So he's your assistant?"

Alex made a face. "Sort of. I was supposed to be mentoring him. I must say, though, his fighting skills surprised me. He has more potential as a guardian angel than I thought."

"Alex, do you think Rob is gay?"

He shrugged. "I've no idea. Why?"

She made a non-committal sound. "Marcie thought he might be. But he seemed awfully interested in Reena."

"It could have been part of his cover." Alex thought of what Michael had said but didn't share that bit of information. After all, things didn't always turn out as planned.

"I suppose."

"Don't start planning on attending their wedding if that's what you're thinking about. I'm not sure if they'll even remember us after all the mind wipes are done."

The elevator stopped and the doors slid open. Alex moved his hand to rest in the small of her back as they made their way down the hall to her apartment. "Right. Mind wipes. You know, I'm still having trouble believing everything you told me."

"I tried to explain as best as I could given that you were being constantly checked by doctors and nurses." Alex took the key from her hand and unlocked the door. "And then later on, we were surrounded by cops. Not exactly conditions conducive to a clear explanation." He stepped aside for her to enter.

"So you're really not human?" Emma took off her coat and hung it up, leaving Alex to close the door behind them.

"No. Like I said, I'm your guardian angel."

She widened her eyes in disbelief. "You said that back at the club. But… An angel? Wings and halo and all that jazz?"

"Wings, yes, but the halo's only for ceremonial occasions." He quirked an eyebrow at her. "I could use a drink. How about you?"

"Best idea I've heard today, but only a very small glass for me, please. Concussion, remember?" She turned on the Christmas tree, its cheery glow matching her mood for the first time in what seemed like ages.

He took a bottle of wine out of the rack and looked around for a corkscrew.

Emma opened a drawer next to the sink and handed him the opener before taking down two glasses from the cabinet above. "Back to the angel stuff. You're kidding me, right? You really have a halo? Where do you keep it, in your sock drawer?" She couldn't keep the gurgle of laughter from bursting out with her words.

Alex grinned as he poured the wine. "Ah, no, I keep it in my locker at work, together with my robes."

"Work?"

He pointed toward the ceiling then handed her a glass. Their fingers brushed, a delicious warmth tingled up her arm and curled around her heart. Emma sighed contentedly but a glance at Alex's face had that warmth cooling. The teasing look had faded from his face and his tone turned serious. "Emma, we have to talk."

"Isn't that what we're doing?" She tried to hold onto the light atmosphere they'd been enjoying.

"Yes, but there are things I have to explain. Serious things." He took her hand and led her over to the couch. "Sit down."

A sense of foreboding came over her. "This isn't going to be good, is it?"

"Emma, please, just let me talk. Don't say anything until I finish. Okay?" Alex took up a stance near the fireplace.

She nodded and took a gulp of her wine thinking she might need some liquid sustenance.

"First of all, let me give you some background. Brace yourself, it's quite an info dump."

"I'm ready." She clasped her fingers tightly around her glass.

He took a sip of his wine and then began. "I've never been human. Angels are created as higher beings and we take on different jobs from the beginning; that is we're trained from the moment we…well, from the moment we emerge. I've been a guardian for about three millennia." Alex set his glass down on the mantel and began to pace. "In all that time I have never been involved with any of my charges on a physical level as I have been with you. I broke a lot of rules when we made love. I'm supposed to come in, save the day, and leave. Befriending is allowed but not interacting on such an intimate level." He took a deep breath but before he could continue, Emma interrupted.

"Wait…backtrack. You've never been physical with any of your charges? Does that mean you were a virgin when we met?"

Alex's eyes creased at the corners. "Er, no. Guardians can be physical with each other; there are no rules against us having relationships within the firm."

"Oh." Her mouth opened to ask another question but he raised a warning finger and she pressed her lips together.

"I don't kiss and tell."

"How did you know…?" She lowered her brows. "Can you read my mind?"

"I wish!" He smiled and sat down beside her. "We don't read minds but we do have the power to wipe the memories of our human charges, and it was done to you and those around you after I was shot but, for some reason, it didn't work on you."

"Of course it didn't work. How could I possibly forget the man I love?" She leaned back on the sofa and rolled her eyes. "Perhaps you can wipe a memory but you can't wipe a heart." She reached out and stroked his cheek.

He moved away ever so slightly and she allowed her hand to drop to her lap, trying not to show her hurt over the fact that he was shunning her touch. What was going on?

"My boss allowed me to come back to you but only under certain conditions."

Emma raised a brow in question but didn't interrupt.

"I wasn't allowed to touch you. I broke that rule—multiple times." He sighed heavily. Leaning forward, he braced his forearms on his knees and stared across the room. "The punishment is harsh. Every time I touched you I moved further into a state called a shade, until finally I became corporeal. Like I am now."

"But you were before. You had to have been, I touched you. You ate and drank. We made love." She reached out to touch him again and this time he didn't rebuff her. She laced her fingers around his arm, thinking how right it felt.

"Yes, but it was a façade." He turned his head to look at her. "I was a guardian angel acting a part. Now I'm human. I no longer have use of my wings or any of my former powers."

"So between the time you pretended to die and now…? What were you doing then?"

"Well…I was in a lot of trouble for taking that bullet." He sat up straight, shifting so he was facing her and took her hands in his. "You were…" He paused and swallowed hard. "You were supposed to die. I intervened with fate."

"I was supposed to die?" A cold wave washed over her. "Did you know that?"

Alex nodded and squeezed her fingers. "I'm usually sent in to save my clients but this time I was only supposed to offer comfort and support during your final days. Once I got to know you, to love you, I couldn't let it happen."

Her thoughts were racing and she stumbled over her words. "I…I don't know what to say. Thank you hardly seems sufficient."

"There's no need. All in a day's work for a GA."

"My hero." She leaned forward and pressed a kiss to his cheek. He smiled and then exhaled loudly.

"Anyway, my supervisor raked me over the coals for interfering and told me I could only watch over you as a spirit, a kind of ghost, and that was only because I'd been given special permission." He made a face. "I'm not very good with following the rules. Because I touched you, kissed you, held you, the rest of the punishment will now be carried out."

"What's the rest of the punishment?"

Alex looked down at their joined hands. "I have twenty-four hours and then I'll just cease to exist."

"Cease…?" She felt the blood drain from her face. "No more second chances?" Her voice cracked as she finished asking. Alex was already shaking his head sadly. Tears stung her eyes and she blinked to hold them at bay.

"No." He sighed and pulled his hand free of hers. He rose to his feet and walked to the Christmas tree, standing with his back to her for a moment. The bit of plastic mistletoe they'd kissed under was hanging there and she watched as he turned slightly to gently nudge it with his finger. She could see the corner of his mouth curve upward in a reminiscent smile then his hand dropped to his side and he turned to face her. "It's the price I had to pay to save your life." His gaze met hers, intense, filled with love and conviction. "And I'd do it all over again just to know you're alive."

"Alex…" Words failed her as the depth of his love hit home. He'd given up eternity just for her. Why? There was nothing special about her. She was just an accountant! What had she ever done to be worthy of such a sacrifice?

Sacrifice.

The enormity of what was happening – what would happen – began to sink in. She blinked trying to hold back tears, her body beginning to shake with reaction. Taking a deep breath, she fought to gain control. She had to be strong for Alex.

With extreme care, Emma put her glass on the side table then stood up. Keeping her eyes locked on his, she moved to where he stood and put her hands on his chest. She spread her fingers wide, absorbing the warmth of his body. He felt so solid and strong. How was it possible that he could die? She felt a wayward tear drip down her cheek as she looked up at him. "How long do we have?"

"Twenty-four hours from the fight at the club." He wiped the tear from her cheek then rested his hands lightly on her waist. There was a sheen in his eyes as he studied her features, as if he were memorizing them. "I'll be leaving the human world, and I'm guessing Heaven as well, at some point tonight, probably sometime before dawn."

Very slowly, Emma brought her hands up to cup his cheeks, her fingers trembling as they touched his skin. "It's Christmas Eve. We've spent almost the entire day dealing with the fallout from Montrose and his sick business." She leaned forward and kissed him, just a soft touch of her lips on his. "Let me take you to bed. If you're going to disappear from my life forever, then I need to store up some memories." She pulled back and pressed a finger to his mouth to stop him from speaking. "No, don't tell me about mind wipes, because they just won't work on me. You will stay in my heart for the rest of my life."

With his hand in hers, she led him into her bedroom. She didn't bother to turn on the light, she could see him in her mind's eye, feel him with her hands and lips. Besides, between the faint glow from lamps outside and the light from the Christmas tree in the living room there was more than enough illumination. By the end of the night, she'd know every inch of his body and it would be indelibly mapped on her heart to comfort her during the lonely years ahead.

The zipper on his hoodie made a soft metallic hissing sound as she pulled it down. Stepping close enough to him that she could feel the heat of his chest through the material of his shirt, she pushed the sweater off his shoulders and let it fall to the floor.

When he moved to touch her, she shook her head and he let his arms drop to his side. She smiled up at him, then, lifting her face she nibbled at his chin and jaw while her fingers dealt with the buttons on his shirt. Soon that garment joined its fellow at their feet.

She rested her hands on Alex's chest, his nipples hard against her palms, and looked up at her angel. His eyes were half closed, watching her closely. She could feel a purr of satisfaction rising from his chest.

Trailing her fingers down his abs, she pressed a kiss to chest. "You're definitely not built like one of those little cupid angels. No round belly," she commented, referring to a long ago conversation.

He gave a soft huff of laughter. "Thank heavens."

"And," she snuck one hand around to squeeze his butt, "nothing chubby about this."

Alex shook his head and, lacing his fingers through her hair, drew her up for a tender kiss.

"You know," she murmured against his lips, "I'd still love you even if you did look like a cupid."

"Right."

She pulled back and looked him in the eye. "I mean it. I love you, Alex. More than I ever thought possible. I love you so much it hurts in here." She pressed a hand to her chest.

"Oh, Emma." He sighed her name and pulled her into a tight embrace.

For a moment they stood like that, her head cradled to his shoulder, arms wrapped around each other. Emma slowly stroked his back, feeling the indent of his spine, the smoothness of his skin, the… Her questing hands paused as they encountered an unexpected ridge. Not his shoulder blades. She frowned. A scar?

"What's that from?" She pulled away.

"What?"

"This." She traced the raised line and Alex cursed softly.

"My wings. Or what remains of them."

"Your wings?" Curious, she slipped around behind him. Near each shoulder blade was a long thin slit. She traced it with her fingertip and he shivered. "Did I hurt you?" She jerked her hand away.

"No. It's just sensitive."

"Oh. So you used to have wings attached there?"

"I still do, though they're pretty shabby now; a side effect of becoming corporeal, and as I said earlier, I can't fly anymore." He hesitated, then shrugged. "I could show you, if you'd like."

She nodded, curious as to how wings could sprout from a man's back.

Alex frowned as if concentrating and then, just as he'd said, a pair of wings emerged. They weren't the gloriously full white wings she'd been expecting. Instead they were thin, bedraggled rather like those of a tree top angel that had seen better days. Even as she watched several feathers drifted to the ground while the wings themselves seemed to fade away before her very eyes.

"They're…gone." She shifted her shocked gaze from where his wings used to be, to his face.

Alex gave a sad smile. "I guess that means I'm officially not an angel anymore. No wings."

"I'm sorry." She felt tears welling in her eyes as she contemplated all he'd lost, just for her.

"No need. I meant what I said, I'd do it all over again to keep you safe." He drew her close, brushing the tear from her cheek with his thumb.

Leaning into him, she offered him her comfort while absorbing his warmth. He caressed her slowly, gently and she did the same appreciating the feel of him, the strength that seemed to emanate from him. Long, slow strokes that eventually morphed into the heat of desire. Daringly she moved her hands to his belt and then traced the bulge below. When he groaned, she smiled and repeated the gesture.

"Emma…"

"Alex…" She teased. Looking up at him, she undid his belt and the button fly of his jeans. When the material finally parted, she let gravity slowly slide his jeans down the length of his powerful legs, and dropped her gaze to the evidence of his desire.

She reached out, touched him, felt the heat of him. She did this to him. It was a heady knowledge, one that gave her an unexpected boldness.

The bed was but a step away and so she nudged him backwards until he sat and then pushed against his chest, forcing him to lie down. One corner of his mouth twitched but he did her bidding. She almost laughed; she wasn't some femme fatale who controlled a man with a single look. She couldn't force Alex to do a single damn thing. He was allowing her to call the shots. But that was okay, while he was acquiescent she was certainly going to take advantage of the situation.

Emma leaned over him, running her hands over his body and then retracing the path with her mouth. She nibbled and licked watching with pleasure as he quivered in response. His musky scent, the salty taste of him… It was like an aphrodisiac; warm, wet heat blooming within her. Lost in the feelings generated by her actions, she started when she felt Alex's hands on her head, his fingers threading through her hair.

Responding to the gentle pressure against her head she looked up.

Alex's voice sounded hoarse. "Take off your clothes. Let me see you."

Rising to her feet, she did as he bid. She'd never felt particularly sexy when undressing in front of a man but Alex's unwavering gaze on her made her feel sensuous. While she divested herself of her clothes he quietly removed the rest of his but remained seated on the edge of the mattress.

Unashamed, Emma stood before her angel and let him look his fill. She could almost feel his eyes tracing over her, lingering on her breasts, the curve of her hips, the juncture of her thighs. Her breath quickened and when he finally held out his hands to her, she was sure her heart would beat out of her chest. He urged her to straddle his lap and, with his strong arms behind her back to steady her, she brought her knees up on either side of him. She could feel the length of him trapped hot and hard between them, pressing against her stomach.

Rising up on her knees she felt him slip into place at the entrance to her body. All she needed to do now was lower herself onto him. But she waited. She teased them both with the gentlest of movements while she kissed and nibbled his lips. His mouth opened beneath hers and his tongue licked at the seam of her lips, requesting entry. Gladly, she gave permission and as he caressed the warm interior of her mouth she lowered herself onto him, encompassing him in her heat.

Wanting to make the moment last, she began to move with incredible slowness, needing to feel everything in detail. This night would have to last her a lifetime.

After a moment, Alex lay back on the bed and took her with him flipping them over as he did. His body pressed hers to the mattress. Never before had she felt so loved as he took charge and, with intense tenderness, moved within her. This wasn't a frantic coupling, or a simple sex act. No, it was a dedication of the soul. And when completion came, as it did for both of them, it came with a rush of love and caring and friendship. Emma was certain she would never know its like again no matter how long she lived.

Afterwards, Alex held her in his arms. She felt she should speak to him—tell him how much she loved him, that she would never forget him—but the words wouldn't come. Instead she pressed against his length, her head over his heart. His hands were stroking her hair, her back, her hip, calming her, soothing her.

"Alex," she sighed, pressing a kiss to his chest just before sleep overtook her.

Chapter 17

Alex shifted position slowly, trying not to wake the woman lying in his arms. A little manoeuvring and he was able to see his watch in the light seeping in from the Christmas tree. He wasn't sure when his final twenty-four hours had begun. The fight had taken place around two in the morning. It was now just after one.

He hadn't slept. He hadn't wanted to waste a minute. With his arms around the woman of his dreams…the last woman he would ever know…he tried to remember every moment they'd spent together over the past month or so. Such a short time in his vast life span but they were the most important weeks of his existence.

What would it feel like, to die? Would it happen in an instant or would Michael make him suffer? He hoped it wouldn't be bad; he didn't want Emma to see him in pain.

An intense feeling of contentment and lethargy crept over him and he fought it. He didn't want to sleep. He needed to meet his destiny head on with eyes wide open.

He blinked and shook his head as his vision blurred. His breathing seemed to slow and his limbs felt heavy. His thinking was sluggish, vague thoughts and memories flitting through his mind. There was that tingling sensation again. Something was off…

"Sorry for breaking the rules, Sir." The words slurred from his lips. "Please, take care of Emma. Let her be happy." Against his will, his grip on her loosened and his eyes closed.

~~~
~~~

Emma awoke the next morning, blinking sleepily. She was on her side facing the window, sun streaming in, reflecting off the dust motes that floated in the air. Lacy fingers of frost edged the panes and in the distance she could hear church bells ringing.

It was Christmas Day.

In years past she'd have jumped out of bed and hurried to look out the window, then, after donning her favourite fuzzy bathrobe and slippers, she'd have made her way to the kitchen to fix a cup of tea before sitting by the Christmas tree to call her mother. But not today.

Her first thought upon waking had been that her life would never be the same again. The joy of Christmas was gone for her. Instead, the festive occasion would be forever associated with the day her heart had died.

She didn't roll over. She didn't want to see the empty space beside her. Alex was gone and all she had was the memory of their perfect night together. She pressed her face to her pillow, willing back the tears that stung her eyes. No crying, she told herself. Alex wouldn't want her to cry over him.

It was useless.

Sobs shook her shoulders as she gave vent to the pain inside.

"Oh, Alex. I already miss you so much."

"Emma?" A sleep-roughened voice spoke behind her and she felt a hand stroke her arm.

With a cry of surprise she rolled over to see Alex lying beside her, a frown marring his brow.

"Alex?" She breathed his name, unable to believe he was there. "You're still here?"

He scrubbed his eyes and cleared his throat. "Yeah. I…I guess I am."

"But how?" She reached out to stroke his cheek. It felt warm and wonderfully familiar.

"I've no idea." The look of wonder on his face slowly transformed into a grin. "But I sure am glad I'm here." He pressed a kiss to her palm.

With a laugh she threw herself into his arms, showering kisses on him which he returned with equal fervour.

After a very satisfying interlude she snuggled in his arms. "I'm so happy I could burst."

"Me too, except…"

She drew back and looked up at him. "Except what?"

"Something is jabbing me in the ribs." He let go of her and fished around under the covers only to pull out a small gift-wrapped package. "From you?"

"Not me." Emma sat up and took it from him, turning it over so she could see the tag. "It says 'To E and A from M.' Who's M? Not Peter Montrose!" She dropped the package as if it were poison.

Alex sat up. "No, definitely not him, the police have him firmly locked up. But I do have a sneaking suspicion."

"Is it safe to open, do you think?"

"Probably. But just in case, let me be the one to unwrap it." He cautiously undid the bow and removed the paper revealing a small, flat, gold box.

Emma bit her lip. "Be careful. It could be one of those weird terrorist packages you hear about on the news. There could be poisonous dust in it or maybe a scorpion."

"I really doubt that but if it will make you happy…" He held the box out at arm's length. Emma gripped his shoulder and cringed as he gingerly removed the lid.

Nothing happened.

"See? Safe." He set the box down on the covers and pulled away the tissue paper that guarded whatever was inside.

Emma exhaled the breath she'd been holding. "Good. So what is it?"

"It's a deck of cards."

"What? Let me see." She reached into the box and took out the elastic wrapped bundle. "It is a deck of cards. How strange." She poked about in the packaging and found a piece of paper. "There's a note."

Alex unfolded it and scanned the message. "Play the rest of your hand carefully and be sure to follow the rules. –M."

Alex frowned. What did Michael mean by that? As he considered the cryptic comment, he suddenly noticed Emma wasn't moving. In fact, she seemed frozen in place. He reached towards her only to hear a voice behind him.

"Merry Christmas, Alex."

With a start, he looked up to see his former superior sitting in a chair near the end of the bed.

"Michael? What are you doing here?" Alex twitched the covers to ensure Emma was properly covered.

"Just checking on a former employee. I want to wish him well in his new life."

"New life? So this is real?"

The corner of Michael's mouth twitched as if he were amused. "Yes, it's real. You've been given a Christmas gift, Alexander. You're fully human."

Alex couldn't contain the grin he felt spreading over his face. "That's great. Do I dare ask why?"

"You've served as a GA for quite some time, one of the best in the squadron as a matter of fact." Michael eased back in his seat. "I had noticed, however, a subtle change in you. A certain weariness, maybe the beginnings of burnout. I knew you needed a change so I sent you to Emma."

"But why not just make me human right away?"

"The gift of humanity isn't given lightly."

"You were testing me by putting Emma's life in danger?" He frowned.

"Not testing, exactly. More like checking your suitability for such a dramatic change. As I told you before, humans and angels have free will. At any point you could have chosen to save yourself and remain a GA. You didn't."

"So...?"

"Self-sacrifice deserves a reward. Emma was willing to give her life for you. You gave up eternity to save her, to see her live a long life. The end result is that you now get to spend the rest of your Earthly lives together."

Together. Alex liked the sound of that. He and Emma could marry, have a family… A grim thought crossed his mind and he frowned. "You told me Emma was scheduled to die. Is that still going to happen?"

"Everyone dies eventually, Alex. You might recall, however, I never said *when* she would die."

"Any hints?"

Michael pursed his lips and appeared deep in thought for a minute, then gave a nod. "I can't be specific but suffice to say the two of you will likely not be talking to me again for quite some time. If you play your cards right, that is."

A feeling of contentment settled over Alex; a knowledge deep inside that spending his life with Emma was exactly where he was meant to be. Whatever came their way in the future, they'd face it together.

"Thanks, Michael, for everything." He extended his hand to shake and then drew back, recalling the last time his palm had connected with the archangel's. That was what had started the whole turning into a shade business, he was sure of it.

Michael chuckled not seeming in the least offended. "One last thing, Alex. Actually, two last things. First of all, Emma will probably need to go job hunting. There will be an in-depth police investigation of Montrose's business dealings; Stapleton, together with his partners, will be caught in their net. Secondly, there's a package next to Emma's computer with all the documentation needed for your new life. And don't thank me. I'm just the messenger. It's the Boss who's ultimately responsible."

"Right." Alex flicked a look upwards and whispered a thank you.

When he looked back towards the end of the bed, the chair was empty and Emma was no longer frozen in place. She was removing the elastic around the cards, seemingly unaware of what had just transpired around her.

Alex glanced at the note one more time and noticed a post script seemed to have appeared out of nowhere. He read the message again. "Play the rest of your hand carefully and be sure to follow the rules. – M. P.S. Beware of accepting handshakes from archangels." Chuckling at his supervisor's sense of humour and minimalistic explanation, he looked up at the woman who held his heart in her very capable, very lovely hands.

"*Who* is this M person? And what does that message mean?" Emma questioned as she took the note to read it for herself.

"Michael."

"Michael? Michael *who*?" She rolled her eyes. "I'm starting to sound like an owl, saying 'who' all the time!"

"Michael, the archangel."

Her mouth opened to form a perfect 'O'.

Laughing, Alex leaned forward and kissed her. "Don't look so surprised. I told you about him last night."

"You told me lots of things last night. I think I stopped listening halfway through."

"That's okay. Even if you had been listening the entire time, I'm sure your enquiring mind would still come up with a ton of questions."

"You're probably right." She murmured her response, now sorting through the cards. "I wonder what game this deck is for. It only has aces and face cards." She held them up for him to see.

A broad grin slowly spread over his face. "Emma, you and I are going to have a long and happy life together."

"What? How do you know? Oh, who cares!" She tossed the cards into the air and wrapped her arms around him. "Merry Christmas, Alex."

"Merry Christmas, Emma."

And as the cards drifted down around them they sank onto the pillows to celebrate as only two lovers can.

~Fin~

In The Cards

Keep reading for two bonus short stories
from Nicky Charles.

Silent Night, Lonely Night

Have you read Nicky Charles' Law of the Lycans series? This is a short story from that series. Nicky wrote this several years ago. Please note it occurs <u>before</u> Betrayed: Days of the Rogue. Damien has just lost Beth and his unborn child. This is how his first Christmas after that horrific event might have unfolded.

Damien hunched his shoulders against the cold wind that stole his breath and reddened his cheeks before swirling down the nearly deserted main street. Snowflakes, mixed with bits of ice, stung his face and clung to his lashes, blurring his vision. He blinked irritably but trudged on, the slush underfoot soaking his feet. He didn't have boots and his toes were growing numb.

Damien, why didn't you dress properly for this weather? Beth's voice echoed in his head, scolding him as she pulled off his wet socks and chafed his frozen feet in her warm hands.

A smile drifted over his face as he imagined how the scene would unfold until they were both warming themselves in bed.

Bed.

Weariness, soul deep, had settled on him, the winter chill sapping his energy. He should find a place to spend the night, but it seemed too much of an effort. Curling up in an alley and drifting off into oblivion would be much easier. There were worse ways to die than hypothermia, he mused. His steps slowed and he eyed the narrow space between two buildings. It really didn't matter to anyone if he lived or died…

Damien!

He forced himself to move, Beth's reprimand sounding in his head. She wanted him to keep going, and for her he would. For her he would do anything.

A door opened to his right, its sensors having detected his presence. He paused as light and warmth spilled out onto the frozen street, pushing back the darkness, beckoning him to come closer. Snatches of Christmas carols filled the air and his nose tingled from the scent of ginger and cinnamon. Reaching out, he caught the handle as the door began to close, for some reason drawn to the interior of the building.

The bell above the door jingled merrily as it closed behind him, blocking the bitterness of the wintery night while at the same time sealing him into the epitome of a Christmas wonderland.

Plastic reindeer and grinning elves adorned the shelves. Garland and twinkling lights were draped over the windows and wrapped around posts. A trio of mechanical snowmen waved and sang while a miniature train driven by Santa wove its way through a tiny village. Damien stared at the display. He hadn't even realized the season. It was Christmas.

I love Christmas. Baking cookies, decorating the tree. Beth smiled at him, her dove grey eyes bright with excitement.

Christmas.

His heart clenched in pain. He'd never shared a Christmas with Beth. She'd been taken from him months before.

We'll go see my parents. They're so anxious to meet you! She'd held his hands, squeezing them tightly, reassuring him when he'd expressed his doubts.

He twisted his lips into a bitter smile. Beth's parents hadn't welcomed him with open arms. Instead they'd accused him of being responsible for their daughter's death. They were right, of course. It had been his fault. He hadn't been there to protect her. Hadn't been able to save her…

"Excuse us."

Someone spoke behind him and Damien stepped further into the store to let the young couple behind him enter. Automatically he noted their appearance, years of training taking over. Mid-twenties. Hand-knitted caps. Older coats. The man had his arm wrapped around the woman's shoulders. She was looking up at him, her eyes filled with adoration while one hand rested on her rounded belly.

A baby.

Regret sliced through him as he thought of the baby he'd never held. His child, killed along with his mate. Everything he'd ever loved had been taken from him.

Frozen in place by grief and regret, he watched the young couple as they moved down the aisle, their feet thumping gently on the old wooden floorboards. It was a small store and he could easily follow their progress. He watched the red pompom on the woman's cap as it bobbed with every step she took. A silly bit of adornment that Beth would have loved.

"Would you like some hot apple cider?" A store clerk seemed to appear from nowhere, a steaming styrofoam cup in her hand. He studied the offering and then looked up at her. She was smiling at him, nodding encouragingly. "It's very good."

"Thanks." He took the cup and drank, surprised at how the sweet liquid slid down his throat and seemed to force the coldness out of his body.

"We have cookies, too." She extended a plate. "It's almost closing time so take as many as you want."

His stomach growled just then and she laughed.

"Here, take the lot of them. I doubt there'll be any more customers with that snowstorm outside. Most people will be heading right home. No one wants to get stuck at work on Christmas Eve."

Damien took the food she offered, befuddled by the generosity. Most places he went, his reception was anything but warm.

"Ten minutes until closing time, if I can help you with anything...?"

He shook his head and she smiled at him again before hurrying over to the cash register, where several customers were now lined up.

Taking a bite of one of the cookies, Damien glanced around, spotted the red pompom a few aisles over and headed in that direction. For some reason, he was curious about the couple, wondering what they were doing on Christmas Eve.

The young woman was lingering by a small display of jewellery. Damien busied himself at a nearby rack, trying to look interested in neckties while watching her out of the corner of his eye. She tried on a silver bracelet adorned with delicate filigree snowflakes, a smile spreading over her face as she examined how it sparkled in the light.

"Kevin, isn't this pretty?" She called over her shoulder to the young man as he emerged from the next aisle.

He nodded, his eyes moving from the bracelet to her face. "It looks beautiful on you. Would you like—?"

But she was shaking her head even before he finished speaking. "No. We can't afford it."

"Maybe I could—"

"No." She pressed her fingertips to his mouth. "We need a new vacuum. I won't have our child crawling around on filthy floors." Sliding the bracelet off, she returned it to the display.

The man wrapped one arm around her shoulder and gave her a hug. "One day, I'll get a better job and I promise I'll shower you with jewels then."

"No need." She stood on tiptoe and kissed him. "You and the baby, that's all I need to make me happy. Now come on, let's go buy a vacuum." Tugging at his arm, she led him away. "I hope they aren't all sold out. It was a great price…"

Damien stepped forward and picked up the bracelet the young woman had been looking at. Holding it to the light, he watched how the snowflakes gently swayed and glistened. It was delicate and beautiful, just like Beth had been. He knew she would have loved it.

He'd never had the chance to buy her a Christmas present, but this would have been the perfect one. The metal warmed in his hand. In his mind's eye, he imagined how he'd kiss her awake and then slide the bracelet around her wrist. She'd smile at him, her eyes sparkling with joy. Then she'd reach up, wrap her arms around his neck and pull him down onto the mattress, thanking him with sweet kisses…

"The store will be closing in five minutes. Please bring your purchases to the front. We thank you for doing your Christmas shopping with us and wish you the happiest of holidays."

The voice on the PA system interrupted his daydream and Damien gave a start, surprised he was in the store and still had the bracelet in his hand.

He fingered the bit of silver again before nodding and heading to the cash register.

"You found something?" The clerk who had given him the cider and cookies smiled at him.

"I..." He stared at the bracelet not sure why he was buying it.

Behind him he could hear laughing. "Kevin, you are such a goof!"

"Sir?" The clerk prodded him. "Do you want a gift box for the bracelet?"

"How much are vacuums?"

If the woman was surprised by his question, she didn't show it. "They're on sale this week." She quoted him the price.

"Good. I'll buy a vacuum and this bracelet." Damien pulled some bills out of his pocket. "This should be enough."

"I'm sure it is." She stared at the pile of cash and reached for the intercom. "I'll just call for someone from the stockroom to bring a vacuum up to the front."

"Never mind. Here comes the vacuum. And give this," he set the bracelet down on the counter, "to her." He jerked his chin towards where the woman with the pompom hat was emerging from the aisles, the man behind her carrying a large box with a picture of a vacuum on it.

"Oh!" The clerk looked from him to the young couple. "Do you know—"

"No." He shook his head. "Just wish them a Merry Christmas."

Without looking back, he left the store.

The snow was still falling when he stepped outside, but it had lost its icy sting. Now, large fat flakes floated down as gently as feathers, caressing his face, coating the world in a soft white blanket.

As he walked down the street, he could hear carols coming from a nearby church, Christmas lights shone from rooftops and trees; strange how he hadn't noticed them earlier.

"Ho, ho ho! Merry Christmas!" A thin Santa stood on the corner, ringing a bell with a collection kettle beside him.

Damien nodded and forced his mouth into a half smile. It wasn't as hard as he'd thought it would have been. He reached into his pocket to pull out some money to give to the man.

"Thanks." The Santa gave him a considering look. "Would you like to join me at the Mission? We're having a Christmas Eve dinner; turkey and all the trimmings."

Damien studied the Santa. There was no pity or scorn on his face, just patience as he waited for an answer.

From some distance away, he heard laughter and, turning his head, he could see a man pulling a child on a sled, shrieks of excitement filling the air.

"Faster, Daddy. Faster."

Daddy.

Those words would never be uttered to him. His child, his family, was dead. Buried in a cold grave. He'd been too late to save them. His fault.

"No." Damien turned back to look at the Santa.

"Are you sure? There are a few spare beds if you feel inclined to wait the storm out someplace warm."

Damien shook his head and turned away. He was a rogue, destined to spend his days roaming the world by himself. Trying to do anything else only ended up hurting others.

Shoving his hands in his pockets, he hunched his shoulders against the icy cold and walked into the night alone.

~Fin~

Gwyneth's Christmas by Nicky Charles

In Betrayed: Book Two – The Road to Redemption, a minor character was introduced. Her name was Gwyneth and she was the owner of Club Mystique. She reappeared in for the Good of All and then niggled my muse into writing a Christmas story for her. She's still not satisfied and it appears that my next novel will need to centre around her if I am to ever get any peace and quiet! -- Nicky

Gwyneth managed to keep the sneer from her face as she murmured an indistinct reply to the patrons that wished her 'Merry Christmas'. Fools, she thought as she watched them file out of her establishment singing snatches of carols. Commercial hype, that's all the day was about.

"Want me to stay and help clean up?" Rudy, the bouncer, came to stand beside her. A wall of muscle, he was, in reality, a gentle giant.

"Thanks for the offer but I'll take care of it. The place is closed tomorrow and I have nothing to do."

"No family to celebrate with?" He frowned. "You could spend the day with me and my wife."

"Rudy." She folded her arms, brows arched in disbelief.

"Sorry. I forgot you don't get into holidays and such." He gave her a repentant grin.

"You're forgiven. Head home. I'll lock the place up."

"Thanks, Gwyn. Have a Merry…er…have a nice night."

Gwyneth shook her head and shut the door firmly behind the bouncer as he left. After flipping the locks and sliding the deadbolt into place, she paused to look out the window. The streets were almost deserted now. She could see Rudy walking down the sidewalk, his feet leaving footprints in the slushy snow.

Gotta love winter in the city, she thought. The white shit that fell from the sky didn't stand a hope in hell of surviving the exhaust from a myriad of vehicles. It turned into brown slop the minute it hit the pavement. Whoever wrote about white Christmases obviously didn't live in Chicago.

A snowflake landed on the window right in front of her. For a split second its delicate beauty glistened before her and then, in the blink of an eye, it melted and dripped down the pane like a tear.

Yeah, Christmas was enough to make anyone cry, even a snowflake, she thought to herself as she turned away.

Making her way to the sound booth, she turned off the track of seasonal tunes. Good riddance. The never-ending loop of saccharine songs gave her a headache.

Peace filled Club Mystique. No music, no TV, no clinking of glasses, no shuffling of chairs. No indistinct chatter caused by dozens of voices. Gwyneth felt her tense muscles loosen, her breathing slow. For a moment she stood there, only the sound of her own heartbeat filling the cavernous room.

Quietude was a stark contrast to the noise that usually surrounded her. The calmness allowed a person to relax, to hear their own thoughts.

Her thoughts.

She tightened her lips as she looked about the room. Almost, she could see the ghostly images of the people who had occupied the club only a short time ago. Laughing and smiling, exchanging hugs or small gifts, their merriment had filled the void.

A blink erased the images and once again she saw scattered chairs, dirty dishes, discarded bits of ribbon and wrapping paper. The lack of noise was almost oppressive. She didn't like silence.

"Looks like it's just you and me again, Sven." She glanced at the tattooed skull on her upper arm.

Sven grinned back at her and she gave him a pat.

"Ah, Sven, I can always count on you, can't I?"

Giving a rueful laugh, she strode across the room, shoving in chairs and grabbing a tray of empty glasses from one of the tables she passed. The clicking of her heels echoed through the room, emphasizing that she was the only living creature in the establishment. Well, there might be a mouse or two since Sherman, her cat, was too lazy to do his duty. The day she'd taken him in as a stray she'd told him he had to earn his keep. Four years later, he was still here and had yet to present her with even one rodent. As a matter of fact, he was probably sleeping in the kitchen, too fat from the scraps he mooched to even move.

Stupid cat.

She brushed against the scraggly Christmas tree one of the wait staff had insisted on erecting. The movement caused a bell to tinkle merrily. Had an angel just received its wings? Wasn't that the story: every time a bell rang, an angel got its wings?

"You can thank me later, buddy." She told the anonymous angel.

A few ornaments were hanging precariously and she shifted the tray of glasses so it was balanced against her hip. With her free hand, she moved the balls to safer locations, her fingers lingering on the smooth, polished surfaces. She adjusted the drooping garland as well then took a half step back to admire the effect. The decorations glistened and sparkled in an almost magical way.

The hint of a smile curled the corner of her mouth before she noticed that half the lights were burnt out. Why people went ga-ga over Christmas trees, she'd never understand.

Giving her head a shake, she set the tray of glasses on the bar. There'd be time enough to put them in the dishwasher tomorrow.

Tomorrow.

It would be a long day. The club was closed and she had no particular plans beyond straightening the place up. Perhaps she'd tackle the books. Now there was a fun way to spend the holidays.

One final scan of the room and she shut off the lights before climbing the stairs to her apartment. Flicking on the radio, she grimaced as she realized all the stations were probably playing Christmas carols. The TV stations would also be suffering from the same malady. Christmas movies and cartoons, news stories about goodwill and peace on Earth.

Yeah. Right.

Might as well go to bed.

She brushed her teeth then removed her makeup, giving her face a critical examination in the process. A few wrinkles around her eyes and mouth. Oh well, at least her hair was still a natural red with no signs of grey. And her boobs weren't sagging…much. As for her stomach, well, maybe Santa would give her a tummy tuck for Christmas.

"What do you think, Sven? Do I need to get this old body trimmed and toned?"

She flexed her arm and the skull appeared to shake its head.

"Thanks, buddy. Yeah, you're right. For a woman my age, I look pretty good." She grinned down at the skull, admiring the roses that grew from the top of its head. Red with thorns, of course, just like her.

Once in bed, she plumped her pillow and pulled the covers up around her shoulders. There was a distinct chill in the room and she shivered.

Hey, Santa, cancel the tummy tuck. I need a bed warmer, she decided. Preferably a male with fully functioning parts.

There was a thump and the mattress jiggled. Raising her head, she saw Sherman blinking at her.

"Hey, Santa, that's not exactly what I meant."

Santa didn't respond, naturally. He only visited good girls and she was decidedly *not* good.

"Oh well, Sherman, you'll have to do." She patted the space beside her and the mammoth cat made its way to the indicated spot. It butted its head against her before lying down.

Shifting to her side, she stroked the animal's thick fur and listened to the ticking of the bedside clock. Out the small window, she could see a neon sign flashing to advertise the existence of an all-night pharmacy. Beyond it the moon illuminated the deep velvet blue of the sky. There were no stars, just the moon looking cold and lonely.

"Merry Christmas," Gwyneth whispered to it. Of course, it didn't answer back.

She blinked her eyes and cleared her throat.

Stupid holiday.

Rolling over, she shut her eyes and focused on sleep.

~Fin~

A Message from Nicky and Jan

Thank you for taking the time to read our story. We hope you enjoyed it. If so, please leave us a review, send us an email or drop by our facebook page. We love hearing from our readers

Connect With Us

http://www.NickyCharles.com
https://www.smashwords.com/profile/view/JanG

You can also follow Jan and Nicky on Facebook:
http://www.facebook.com/Nicky-Charles

Or write to:
nicky.charles@live.ca

Our Books

Hearts & Halos
In the Cards
Untried Hearts

Nicky Charles' Law of the Lycans series
The Mating
The Keeping
The Finding
Bonded
Betrayed: Days of the Rogue
Betrayed: Book 2 – The Road to Redemption
For the Good of All
Deceit can be Deadly
Kane: I Am Alpha

Forever In Time (standalone)

Jan Gordon
Black Silk
Life in the Shadows